TRULY

The Missing Diamonds Mystery

CHERIE RASHEL

BRIGHTON PUBLISHING LLC
435 N. HARRIS DRIVE
MESA, AZ 85203

Truly Hidden

The Missing Diamonds Mystery

Cherie Rashel

Brighton Publishing LLC
435 N. Harris Drive
Mesa, AZ 85203
www.BrightonPublishing.com

Copyright © 2013

ISBN 13: 978-1-62183-164-8
ISBN 10: 1-621-83164-7

Printed in the United States of America

First Edition

Cover Design: Tom Rodriguez

DEDICATION

To Him who gives gifts.

PROLOGUE

O h, if I could jog back in time for just a few moments, I would rest in an oversized leather chair that sits next to the fireplace and steal time with the one person who changed my life from our first meeting. And the memory of that revisited encounter would have to last a lifetime. I was too small of a boy when first I met him to realize that what I was experiencing would set about a stream of events that would weave in and out of my very existence for many years to come. Even now my mind tries to draw on every precious, detailed moment of that meeting, thinking hard on the one secretive detail my grandfather shared with only me, a secret that would launch a chain of dramatic events and steer my life down a road of danger until I came to rest exactly where he pictured me to be.

CHAPTER ONE

The Meeting

The turbulence tossed the small plane like a piece of laundry blowing in the wind. The passengers sat dead still. Fear had suddenly weaved itself through the small plane, immobilizing even the youngest passenger.

Peter Armstrong, a nine year old, sat perfectly still beside his mother, Sarah Armstrong, who placed her arm around her son's small shoulders. As the plane lurched, she leaned above him and whispered comforting words into his ear, hoping to calm his young nerves as the plane determinedly began to smooth itself out and push forward along its course. Sarah was Nicholas Armstrong's only daughter-in-law, and Peter was his only grandchild. Nicholas knew he would have to utilize this time wisely; the chance of another visit could not be taken for granted. The plane began its choppy decent, until it finally settled down on a small narrow runway, reaching its destination in Southwestern Africa.

Peter's eyes searched the area outside the small plane window as he clutched an old picture of his grandfather that had been kept for years. The edges were bent and slightly folded. It showed like the wear of an article that had been sought after,

1

handled, and gone back to time and time again. It didn't take but one or two swipes from Peter's young eyes to target the one person who matched the picture.

His widowed grandfather was a man of some age, tall, slightly grayed, and strong. He wore a smile on his face that showed a hidden excitement about the meeting that was about to take place. Peter watched as his mother tightly hugged this man. The expression on their faces couldn't hide the shared remembrance that linked them. Nicholas had lost his son, and Sarah had lost her husband. After their warm exchange, they turned in unison to center their attention totally on Peter. The intensity of their concentration made Peter sink within himself like a turtle in his shell with no place to hide.

"This is Peter," Sarah said to his grandfather, who bent down and offered Peter his hand with gentle kindness. To a boy of Peter's size, his grandfather's hand seemed huge and rough. Peter wanted to be afraid but there was something in the way that his grandfather presented himself to others that melted Peter's nerves and drew from him a genuine fondness that manifested now as a surreptitious smile that flashed across the boy's face.

Nicholas had a stately old house that oozed with manly character. It was built years ago for a local government official and had long ago changed hands. Time had reduced the dwelling to a wonderfully woodworked masculine old home. The house had four huge bedrooms and a gentleman's library. Every room had dark, thick, beautiful woodworking that showed the talent of the master builder. There was a fireplace in every room to help heat the bones of visitors on nights when the chilling dampness of the evening air would hunt them down, penetrating layers of clothing to the very core of their being. The chairs were large and comfortable, nicely placed to catch full advantage of the heat as it emanated from the huge fireplaces.

Weeks went by and the bond that grew between grandfather and grandson became more obvious to everyone who had a mind to notice. There was one relative in particular that seemed to be the most disturbed about the relationship and that was Ken Johnson. Secretively, when he thought eyes were not on him, he would throw disturbing stares in their direction. It was obvious to anyone who could see that Peter's visit created a deep disturbance for Ken.

Ken Johnson was Nicholas's brother-in-law and, as long as Ken had remained married to Ester, Nicholas's younger sister, they maintained a façade of friendship. But after she passed away, there was no longer a relationship left between the two of them. In fact, there seemed to be an increasing animosity between the two men, making it impossible to keep hidden the powerful hatred on Ken's face toward Nicholas, almost like he knew the secret. Nicholas was almost positive that no one could have witnessed the exchange that took place that day, but if someone did see the transaction happen, it only applied an increasing amount of pressure on Nicholas to confide this information to Peter before he left, because he may never see him again.

Several years before the arrival of Sarah and Peter, Nicholas had been working in one of the deeply hidden diamond mines common to the area. The men labored hard in their effort to unearth the precious gems from their hiding places. Once in a while a new strain would show itself after an explosion. The surrounding workers would rush in to help extract any rare beauties. A flash of exhilaration would travel through the men like a shock of electricity when one of the digs would surface a special find. The sparkling gem would hold their attention in awe. Every worker knew that they were not allowed to keep any of the diamonds, large or small, that were unearthed in the mines. It was rumored that anyone caught trying to sneak an unpolished rough diamond out of the mines would be put to death. No one ever actually witnessed another worker being put to death, but some people would suddenly just disappear, probably sent packing after being caught.

The natives who lived in the thick jungle were seldom seen and were feared by most of the local people. If anyone did come across any tribe's people, they would just nod, look down, and keep right on walking. The aggressiveness of the natives had dissipated long ago. The real problem lay in the fears and superstitions that drove the thoughts and actions of the local population. Their fear and superstition were furthered by the refusal of the natives to work in the mines or enter their depths. There seemed to be an imaginary line that forced them to stop in fear at the cave entrances, a behavior believed to have begun when the last time one of the natives went into a mine, he was never seen again. His disappearance drove a deeper fear into the souls of the natives. They were too afraid to enter the cave to search for him, probably for fear of being attacked by bats or some imaginary voodoo curse. Not one volunteer was found to even try. They just waited by the mouth of the cave until one by one they walked away, leaving the unfortunate's beloved behind. She stood there alone and, when she could wait no longer, she too would slowly turn and walk a lonely path home with her head hung low.

The diamonds were not valuable to the natives, but the natives were aware of the fact that their white neighbors put a great deal of worth on them. Because the natives couldn't be enticed with any type of payment, it forced the owners of the mines to hire outsiders to do the work. Their refusal to work was first met with violence between the natives and the boss men, who tried to coerce them to work in the caves. War broke out, and many deaths were recorded, permanently freezing any help from the unwilling natives. The war was costly, and the owners of the mines eventually gave up trying to employ any of the tribesmen either through physical coercion or payment. The natives couldn't be convinced to enter the work area and using physical coercion only led to armed conflict, so the natives were left alone, and the two populations took to ignoring each other, creating an icy peace between them.

It was Sunday, and the miners had this one day to relax and unwind from the busy week of working in the depths of the mines. On these days, Nicholas was eager to spend the day outside and would allow himself a long, tranquil walk. The dusty paths seemed to separate the lush greenery that grew so thick and ramose that it formed an overhead canopy that shaded appreciative travelers from the pounding sun. There were some very special places where Nicholas loved to walk. The beauty of the area seemed to soothe any loneliness or agitation that would surprisingly attack him at times.

It was raining that day but not hard enough to prevent his customary walk, so he grabbed his homemade umbrella and headed toward the waterfalls. His pace was slow and enjoyable, but after walking an hour or so, his serenity was interrupted by the faint sounds of a woman crying in mourning. Slowing his pace, he struggled to determine in which direction the cries were coming from. He stopped to listen more intently. The cries seemed to be coming from an abandoned area where the miners had stopped working years ago when no more diamonds could be found.

Nicholas' curiosity pulled him in the direction of the mourning woman. The moans were like something he had never heard before. As he drew closer, he identified the cries as that of native tribeswoman, who seemed to be growing weaker with exhaustion. Nicholas's mind percolated in wonderment at the cause of her distress. As he rounded the corner, he was completely surprised to see a large group of natives standing around this crying woman. He was puzzled over the fact that there seemed to be no one helping her. Nicholas's first thought was to turn and run but the sobs of the women caught his ear. Instead, he cautiously approached the small clearing. No one turned to look at him. No one cared that he was there. They were too intent on the heart-rending situation. As he slowly approached, he strained to make some sort of sense out of the circumstances that would cause such distress.

The lamenting woman was standing at the mouth of an old mine cave. Nicholas breathed a sigh of relief when he recognized one of the tribesmen. He had seen him at the trading store once in a while and knew he spoke broken English. Slowly he walked up to the man named Jayba, looked him in the eye, and asked him why the woman was crying. Jayba said, "Woman's baby crawled into the cave, and no one here to go in to bring him out." Nicholas stood there in thought for only a moment. He knew the mines were dangerous and the chances for that small child coming out alive, if at all, were very slim.

Very methodically Nicholas walked to the entrance of the mine, strained to focus his eyes in only darkness, and then stepped into the unknown. Walking only a few steps, he stopped to listen but heard nothing. He couldn't see and he couldn't hear any sign of the child that would lead him in the right direction. Taking one-step at a time, securing each foot ahead of himself carefully, he slowly inched forward. Though his eyes adjusted somewhat to the darkness, he could see only a few feet in front of him and only with the light coming from the entrance of the mine. What he didn't see to the left was the small abyss that was deep enough to take a human being down and leave their whereabouts a mystery forever. The area to the left was totally impassable and only along the right wall of the mine could one make their way deeper into its darkness. As beads of sweat began to form on his forehead, the realization nothing but a deep hole lay directly in front of him made him stop and let out a groan. The fear had hit home, and he deliberately took a step back, clutching the wall behind him.

The darkness made forward movement impossible, and he knew that he must go back to get some kind of light or rope if he was going to find the small child. As he exited the caves, the group of natives standing outside the cave stared at him with such haunting looks on their faces that it sent a chill down Nicholas's spine and stopped him dead in his tracks. Deliberately trying to keep control of his thoughts, he quickly formed the only plan that could help them. Nicholas approached Jayba, gesturing for the torch that the tribesman held in his hand. With torch in hand, Nicholas took a deep breath before reluctantly re-entering the cave. The torch illuminated the gaping hole to left of him, which immediately sobered him up with a thought of what would have happened if he had taken another step. He slid to the right and moved slowly along the cold, slimly wall.

He stopped again to listen. This time he heard something deep within the sweating cave. He really didn't want to go any further into such darkness but the thought of those faces, those haunting faces waiting outside of the cave forced him to put one foot in front of the other. The crunching sounds beneath his feet warned him not to look down to see what he was stepping on. Very slowly he inched his way along the wall unaware of how much time had gone by. He stopped to wipe his brow with the back of his hand. "Where could that baby be?" he said aloud in desperation. "I can't give up now."

Then a slight whimpering noise echoed from deep within the mine. Without moving he strained his ears to listen more intently. He heard the noise again and thought that it must be the child. With what little light he had, he strained his eyes and inched deeper into the mine. Before long, the shape of a small child emerged at the edge of the light, sitting dangerously close to the edge of the abyss. With slow, deliberate steps he approached the child, and then bent down in one fell swoop to snatch it up. He held the boy tight, making sure that he wouldn't lose the child in the darkness. Nicholas could feel a penetrating coldness coming from boy's body. He wondered how long he had been in there. Gripping him tighter to help warm the little soul a little better, with his own body heat, he began to make his way back to the mouth of the cave. As he approached the tiny amount of daylight that seemed so far off in the distance, it appeared to be moving back and forth with each step he was taking. Nicholas knew his mind was playing tricks on him. All he wanted to do was get out of the cave with the boy in his arms. He purposely tried to not touch the sides of the cave because of the slimy staleness of the walls. He had to watch his footing—he knew he could fall and lose both himself and the child to the darkness that engulfed them. He whispered a prayer as he moved toward the opening of the cave, which grew larger with each cautious step.

When he reached the cave entrance and stepped out into the open, he took in a deep breath of fresh air just to keep from passing out. He heard the low murmuring sounds of the tribe's people who rushed to take the child from him. Their collective murmur left an eeriness in the air that seared itself into his memory. It would bother him later that day when he relaxed his mind enough to let his memory recall the day's events. Within moments, the tribe vanished. The whole crowd that was there for such a long period of time left without a trace. They just disappeared.

Nicholas stood in the light drizzle for a few minutes until he began to feel the chill of the rain and the strain of the rescue. He was exhausted, and he began looking forward to a nice warm fireplace and a soft bed to rest his bones for a long, undisturbed sleep. Turning slowly, he began the long walk in the direction of his home. *I hope the boy is all right*, he thought to himself. For such a little body, he sure felt cold in my arms. At least Nicholas knew he was alive—and he couldn't begin to imagine how the mother must have felt.

Hours must have gone by before he even moved. Sitting up he couldn't believe the room was beginning to show signs of daybreak. He glanced at the small clock teetering on the edge of the old wooden nightstand next to his bed as he adjusted his tired eyes to read the blurred numbers. He must have slept the entire evening. When his head cleared, he allowed himself time to contemplate the events from the day before. He would have to work hard to put it all in the back of his mind and go on about his day, knowing he would never want to go into that cave again. Just the thought of it made him shiver. The only good thing that came out of all this was that the small child was safe—and hopefully, he was warm and fed sleeping peacefully somewhere.

Nicholas walked the same path to work every day, taking the same route back. The exception was a path that corkscrewed along the river where the wildlife gathered for a quick drink. Occasionally, he liked to take this path home so that he could pause momentarily to watch the setting sun. The purple rays of dusk would send long beams of light between the huge leaves of the giant trees, creating rainbows in the water. An old stump created a perfect chair for him where he sat in complete silence so that he could watch the birds swoop down from the air and ripple the surface of the water as they snatched insects from its surface. Nicholas rested his thoughts, sighing deeply while observing the tranquil drama acted out right before his eyes.

Suddenly his peace was shattered by the sound of leaves cracking on the other side of the river. It sounded like steps pushing dry foliage along. Straining his eyes, he closely watched the opposite bank of the river for any slow-moving shadows sneaking between the huge trees. His senses sent warnings up and down his spine, creating intense apprehension. Someone was there; he knew this for sure because of the sound of small twigs snapping beneath the weight of a moving body. Nicholas remembered the sounds. The same sounds and sensations had disturbed his peace just one week ago, making him nervous enough to increase his pace and shorten his usual walk home. He remembered glancing over his shoulder more times than normal.

He was uneasy. The thought of being tailed was beginning to play on his mind and compelled him to use alternative routes. In spite of his efforts, the sounds persisted. Pondering his problem, he decided to face it head on. With deliberate thought, he made the decision to take his usual route home and just let the circumstances come to pass. *Tomorrow*, he tiredly thought, *tomorrow I'll not take this fear any longer. I'll find out who's following me, and what they have in mind or what they plan on doing.*

Nicholas began his walk home the following day. He restrained himself and purposely walked slower, turning his neck in all directions trying to catch a glimpse of his follower. Each step took him into an agonizing mind spin making his heartbeat a little

11

faster, until he could stand it no longer. Then he heard the sound of footsteps in the forest again. Someone was there and someone was following him. It made him stop dead in his tracks, freezing him in time. He never thought that anything could jolt him to such a degree of panic. *Move*, he thought to himself. *I have to move. I cannot just stand here.* Slowly, he began to walk, keeping a steady pace. Someone was definitely behind him. Fear gripped him, preventing his neck from turning back to get a glimpse of his stalker. Nevertheless, his panic caused his footing to become careless.

The path would ever so often host a smooth tree root that would protrude from the ground and catch inattentive travelers by surprise. Nicholas was pretty sure-footed, but in his nervousness, he never saw the winding root arching upward in the pathway. In his haste, the root grabbed hold of his shoe. Nicholas helplessly fell to the ground, twisting his ankle. He let out a low groan. Blood rushed to his head, causing him considerable confusion. *Get up*, he thought to himself—but forcing his body to rise took all the energy he could muster.

Before he took another painful step, he sensed someone standing behind him. Very slowly he turned to see who it was. To his surprise, he found himself gazing into the eyes of the native women whose child had crawled into the cave. She was just standing there. Every fiber of his body seemed to relax. All the pent up fear began to drain out of him like water slowly running down a drain. Straightening himself upright, he just stood there letting out a sigh of relief. Then he thought of the child and wondered how he might be doing after his ordeal. He knew that the native woman didn't speak English, so he just smiled and nodded at her kindly before turning and limping slowly away.

Before he had gotten too far, the native women walked up behind him and caused him to stop. She then gently placed into his hand two beautifully formed diamonds about the size of two very large grapes. Nicholas slowly raised his hand to see what she had given him. His eyes and mind would not allow him total comprehension of what he was truly seeing. They were exquisite. One was crystal clear and replicated the sunlight. The second diamond was rarest of all. Very few brilliant stones of this shade have ever been found. The stone had a slight trace of teal with an incredible sparkle and an awesome hue. His tired eyes studied the two gems as he tried to understand the meaning of the gift. He turned to her for answers but to his bewilderment she wasn't there. Clearing his weary eyes, he strained to see if the precious diamonds were real.

Breaking the solitude of the moment, a twig cracked across the river and he knew it wasn't the woman. Searching the opposite bank for any sign of who could be there, he didn't see the shadowy figure of a man hiding in the thick brush. After waiting a lengthy period of time to see who would emerge from the woods, he began his painful walk home. Ever so carefully he placed the two diamonds in his right pants pocket and then bent down to grab a thick twisted stick to act as an aid. With each step his ankle made itself known with a deep throbbing ache.

The sleep that overtook him that night was like a narcotic. Sleep came fast and restlessness was not a part of the night's slumber. He hardly moved an inch the entire night. As consciousness gradually began to penetrate his tired mind, forcing him awake, the memory of the day before hit his intellect. *Could it have been a dream?* he thought to himself. The pain from his injured ankle began to tug on his sluggish mind like a distant aching thought, coercing him to full awareness. His mind logically calculated the theory of his pain being true, therefore, so were the diamonds.

His eyelids shot open as he recalled the native women, and then traveling in natural succession, his thoughts focused on the two diamonds. He hoped they were still nicely tucked away in his pants pocket. He whipped his feet out of bed in an effort to land them square on the floor. Slowly and with tremendous pain localized in his ankle, he limped across the room in search of yesterday's clothing, heading directly to where his pants were laid over the chair. His mind needed reassuring, so he reached into his pocket, and ever so gently he pulled out the two things he needed to see, making sure in his mind, that they even existed. There they sat, snuggled together, a hefty weight in the palm of his hand.

Nicholas took his time to admire the feel of them, wondering why the native woman had given him these two invaluable gems. She must have been thanking him for going into the cave that day to rescue her child. Everyone in the area knew the natives had a supply of found diamonds among themselves. They had no use for them but knew enough to store them in a long established hiding place to keep them out of the hands of the dangerous men who would stop at no means to get them. Many foreigners thought they could trick or force the tribe's people into giving them the secret of the diamond vein from which they drew their store or even where the tribe hid their diamonds. Diamond thieves would barely escape the area with their lives and, if they were caught, would never to be seen again. They also found out that telling anyone or sending anyone back might mean death for the intruder, so they kept their mouths shut and never spoke of the diamonds again.

Nicholas stared at the diamonds for a long time before the realization of their great value began to sink in. This comprehension began to make him extremely nervous. Now he had something valuable enough to be guarded. Suspiciously his eyes searched the room and stopped dead when they hit the door. His heart seemed to abruptly stop as he stood there frozen, staring at the entrance. The area appeared to increase in size as it zoomed into view. The fact that the door stood slightly ajar could not go unnoticed.

Suddenly a vague recollection triggered his memory. Someone or some sound woke him from a very deep slumber. Straining his thoughts, he tried to remember what it was that jarred him awake at dawn, sending his mind into an instant rewind. He recalled the noise he heard just before daybreak—the squeak of the door. There was someone in his room while he was sleeping. Nicholas was disturbed with the thought of this intrusion. He didn't see anyone, but sensed that someone had been there.

Quickly turning, his eyes went directly to the two gems now laying side by side in his handkerchief on the old end table. He wondered why they didn't take the diamonds and then realized his sudden start out of bed must have scared them off. An unfathomable fear was beginning to haunt his very thoughts. *What if someone knows my secret?* he wondered. He now realized that whoever it was wouldn't be able to contain themselves. The diamonds were invaluable. Greed would probably overtake them and cause them to become careless and aggressive. He may very well be in a good deal of danger. He deliberately closed, and then locked the door.

A hiding place, Nicholas thought to himself. *I need to find a hiding place for the gems.*

He knew that leaving them in the house would be too dangerous. There wasn't a room in the house that could provide a suitable hiding place. Suddenly it occurred to him how best to keep the diamonds safe from discovery. Methodically, he made his way to the corner of the room to an area beside the door where his old umbrella stand was inconspicuously located. He reached into the crowded container, shifted a few umbrellas moving them out of his way as he searched and found what he was looking for. He pulled out a strong, solid, hickory walking stick. He slowly ran his hand up and down the old, worn cane knowing exactly what he was going to do. Tenderly taking the stick, he placed it carefully on the table and then walked to a drawer to remove his cutting knife. He positioned the blade on a planned spot; and with the movements of a master carver, he steadily applied the knife to an area close to the handle, plucking out small pieces of wood until an oval hole appeared just deep enough to embed his two precious gems.

When the carving was complete, he dropped the two diamonds deep within the oval opening of the stick. Meticulously he mixed an epoxy-like glue and a small amount of wood dust, and then very carefully applied the mixture to the hole until the diamonds were completely hidden. When he was done he purposely rubbed a small amount of dirt directly on the newly applied glue just to hide the freshly changed area. *No one will ever find them now*, he smiled to himself. His sore ankle would provide him with a ready excuse to use his walking stick and keep the diamonds close by his side.

From that day on the people of the village would always see Nicholas with his walking stick. He would force himself to get accustomed to its constant companionship such that it became a third appendage. It not only became a physical part of him, but it also made him appear—and act—more gentlemanly. It gave him incredible peace of mind knowing where the diamonds were at every moment of his day.

Coming home late one evening, before reaching for the doorknob, Nicholas instantly knew something was wrong. At a glance he could see the wood surrounding the hinges was fractured and broken. The door was sitting slightly ajar, and there was a small telltale light forcing its way through the splintered, hinged area of the door. This was the first clue to announce the upheaval before he entered the room. With his mouth hung in disbelief, Nicholas slowly pushed back the broken door, leaving just enough room for him to pass. He could barely believe what he saw. His entire house had been ransacked. The intruders had left not a single inch unturned, unbroken, or untouched. He stood there for some time allowing his mind to process the scene. His diamonds were safe, but it was clear that he was not. Whoever knew his secret did not know where he hid the diamonds but they were willing to ransack his house for them. *Who knew what else they are capable of?* he wondered. He would have to be very careful about where he went and whom he talked to, but leaving his home in Africa was not an option and nothing would drive him away—not even this.

Years went by and the only trouble Nicholas occasionally faced was coming home to a ransacked room and always when he least expected it. This stopped unnerving him long ago because the value of his belongings held no interest for the searcher, so nothing was ever taken. He would put things back in their proper places after being thrown around again and again in a desperate search. A small smile began to grow on Nicholas's face as he thought to himself, *You'll never find them, whoever you are.*

CHAPTER TWO

Revealing the Secret

As the days of their visit began to decrease in number, Peter would confidently beg his grandfather to take him for another walk in the jungle. It didn't take much begging because Nicholas loved to hike and the walks were more enjoyable now because someone he loved went with him. Peter would grab his grandfather's hand and pull him along in his excitement. "Let's go to the pond today, Grandfather," Peter would beg.

At the pond, hundreds of beautifully colored butterflies would lightly dip the top of the water, leaving tiny ripples that looked like little bullseyes. Some of the butterflies were the size of small birds. Their wingspans were as remarkable as their color. Peter and his grandfather would stand there lost in time, watching the iridescent butterflies land on the heated leaves that baked in the sun next to the pond, spreading their wings open and close. It looked like a moving carpet of changing colors.

If they sat there real still and waited for a short while, one elephant after another would parade down to the water's edge for their daily drink. They would carefully step into the mucky edge without a care for the presence of Peter and his grandfather. They would fill their trunks to capacity with water and quickly spray their backsides in an effort to rid themselves of the pestering insects that would constantly attack them. This method had the dual purpose of also cooling their large bodies beneath the hot sun when their fanning ears failed to bring their temperature down. The eye-devouring scene resembled an elephant playground in a water show. Nicholas and Peter would drink in as much as their senses could hold before time forced them to begin their leisurely walk home.

They condensed as much as they were capable of doing into this one day, enjoying each other's company immensely. Their thoughts were anywhere but on the realization that their time together would be drawing to a close very soon. The moment of their departure loomed as a constant shadow in their minds. Peter was unaware that his grandfather was contemplating a time and place to reveal his secret. Nicholas knew he would have to tell Peter in a clear, uncluttered way so he could remember every one of the four detailed instructions that were so important to his future. As the day of Peter's departure grew nearer, Nicholas's feelings grew a little more serious, and he spent a great deal of time in thoughtful planning, dreading that day because it meant their time together would soon be over. There would be only one unscheduled afternoon left before Peter and his mother were to leave. This day would supply all the private time Nicholas would need to convey to Peter how he would acquire the diamonds and receive them in the distant future.

His grandfather gently coaxed Peter into the library, making sure there was no chance of anyone being within hearing distance. Nicholas closed the huge set of double doors behind him.

Peter sat there with eyes wide, wondering what was so important that his grandfather was being so secretive. Nicholas walked over to Peter and motioned for him to sit directly in front of him, so they could be face to face. "Peter," he said, "are you capable of keeping a secret?"

A very serious Peter answered, "Yes, Grandfather. I am very good at keeping secrets."

"That's good," his grandfather replied, "because what I'm going to tell you is a secret, and you cannot tell anyone else, ever. Do you understand what I'm trying to tell you? You cannot tell anyone, Peter. You'll have to keep this a secret." Peter shook his head affirmatively to let his grandfather know he understood.

"Peter," his grandfather began, "if I only knew the future, this would be much easier. I'm not sure I'll ever see you again," he said. "The distance that will stand between us may keep us from ever visiting again. I intend to live the remainder of my life here in Africa. It's become my home now, and I've become very comfortable here. So, what I am going to tell you, you must remember. Are you ready?"

Peter shook his head to let his grandfather know he was listening intently. "Peter, if I ever become sick, I will send you a package containing some of my belongings. If I should die, I will put my attorney in charge of sending you those few treasured items. I have no idea when this will happen but someday it will."

Peter sat there wide-eyed and serious; he soaked in every word his grandfather was telling him.

"Peter, among those items that I will send you, will be my staff." Nicholas walked over to his easy chair to retrieve his walking stick from its resting place against the arm of the chair. He turned and walked back to sit beside Peter. Looking Peter straight in the eyes with a loving expression that only a grandfather could give, he began by telling him the story how he saved the little boy in the cave and how the native women placed two diamonds in his hand.

He told Peter the diamonds were appraised by the Huntington Museum in the states, and the museum has the appraisals on record ready to make a sale. Realizing he was talking to a young boy he simply said that the museum would be willing to buy one or both of them for a very large amount of money. Using his better judgment, he did not relay to Peter that their true worth was somewhere in the seven-digit category. The blue one would be the more valuable of the two.

"Peter," his grandfather whispered, "I haven't an immediate need for the money and your mother was well compensated when your father was killed in the war. That's why she came to live with me before I decided to leave and begin a new life in Africa. Your contact person at the museum is a gentleman by the name of Charles Morgan. He has become my friend and is well aware of the circumstance involving the state of my affairs. He can be trusted to arrange an honest exchange. I have been communicating with him on a regular basis since my last visit to the States. He is a man about six-feet tall with graying black hair. He is a nice looking gentleman with only one distinction of his own—something you should probably be aware of."

Nicholas continued, "Without warning, an unexpected earthquake caused considerable damage to the museum and destroyed the office that belonged to Mr. Morgan. He was sitting at his desk when he felt a swaying movement and a slight vibration. The movement forced him to grab hold of his desk to balance himself while the building began cracking. As each new tremor dealt its blow, Mr. Morgan tried to comprehend the severity of the situation. Rising from his chair, he struggled to walk on the swaying floor. Reaching for the door handle was a normal thing to do but in an earthquake a giant piece of glass from the door split in half and jumped out of its frame. The piece of glass went rushing to the floor with the force of gravity accelerating its descent and cut off the tip of his little finger on his left hand before it smashed to the floor.

He continued to make his way out of the crumbling building, surviving the quake without additional injury. Peter, this Mr. Morgan is the person you should see when you are older. Peter, I also need to stress that there are people who would kill for these two diamonds. That is why it is so important for you to keep this secret." He continued to whisper, "It's all for your own safety, and it's best that no one knows the diamonds will be coming to you. Do you understand what I'm trying to tell you?"

"Grandfather, I can and will keep this secret. I promise, I will tell no one," Peter replied with a look that reflected the perceptiveness of an adult. Peter knew exactly what this giant of a man was trying to tell him. Leaning forward and kissing him on the cheek, Peter whispered, "I love you, Grandpa, and I will never forget you."

His grandfather hugged him close for a long time and then started to tell him the rest of the story. Peter listened as intently as he could, taking in everything his grandfather was saying like a sponge soaking up water. Nicholas slowly looked around the room to make sure no one was eavesdropping before he began. With his hand caressing the cane he was holding, he looked Peter directly in the eye and with his index finger pointed to the spot where it appeared to have a small repair.

"They are right here," Nicolas said as his finger rested on the important spot on the cane. Do you understand what I am trying to tell you, Peter?"

"Yes. They are right there," Peter answered as he pointed to the exact location where the diamonds were snuggly hidden. Nicholas leaned back in his chair, breathed a long sigh of relief, and just lavished in the companionship of his small grandson. They both sat there looking at each other. They both had smiles on their faces and looked like cats that had swallowed canaries. The remainder of their visit was marked by a certain air of camaraderie that was lost upon others. It was their secret to be tucked away in the back of their minds in a special resting place until some memory or event would trigger its presence and pull it forward to be savored as a delectable piece of nostalgia.

CHAPTER THREE

Who's to be Trusted?

The following twelve years passed by slowly, and Peter never forgot his grandfather or the one visit they shared even though the memory of it seemed to fade with the passing of time. Peter was now attending Penn State. He had grown to be a very handsome young man. He was tall and dark and had a smile that could set anyone back a bit. He was hard working, kept his nose to the grindstone, and was in his last year of schooling before he would graduate with honor.

Peter was never at a loss for friends. People were drawn to his charismatic personality and pleasant manner. His smile revealed a sense of humor that drew people to him. Tom was Peter's best friend. They met at college. Tom presented himself as a man of good character at the university. He was honest and intelligent. He was also very confident and popular in his own right. With his wavy blonde hair, he too would turn many heads as he walked down the hall. Yet there always seemed to be a pleasant smile on his face that indicated there was a generally good disposition behind it. Wherever the two of them went, good cheer followed. His friendship with Tom would be the second most important bond Peter would form in his lifetime. In the days to come, Peter would have to trust Tom implicitly because Tom would also know the secret.

Tom's younger sister, Rachel, had shoulder-length, soft, blonde hair, with big brown eyes, and was unaware of the fact that she was an extremely beautiful young woman. Many eyes would turn in her direction, but she never noticed the attention she garnered. The two of them grew up on a farm; it was small but had a variety of animals from which the family fashioned a life. As children, they felt they never had enough time to enjoy the things they really wanted to do. Their parents had a difficult time keeping up with the chores, so by necessity Tom and Rachel helped run the farm. Their efforts never went unappreciated, but the days were long and hard for children of their ages. There were always weeds to pull, eggs to gather, berries to pick, potatoes to dig, pigs to feed, windows to wash, and sometimes snow to shovel. Tom always helped his little sister with her chores after he finished his own responsibilities. She loved her older brother. The work held the family together and created a deep appreciation between each of the members of the family.

Rachel and Tom both had natural artistic ability that seemed to surface and increase as they grew older, and their talents made both of them very inviting students for some of the better colleges and universities in the country. By the time Rachel had left for school, Tom was already a graduating college student, himself. When Tom graduated from college, he obtained a position at Towerton Advertising. He eventually achieved a high level of success.

Rachel too would have success. She and her parents were overjoyed when she was granted an interview at Glass Design Inc., a company that granted interviews only to extremely talented artists. They were less surprised when the company offered her a job because they knew how talented their daughter was. Her artistic temperament allowed her to work wonders in glass, and her determination always lead her to take on challenging projects. Water, for example, was particularly difficult to render in glass but working on such challenging projects gave her a chance to draw out her deepest skill. Her employers loved her work, and her life was good and uncomplicated until one day when Tom phoned to ask her for a favor. Tom had a serious tone in his voice, and when he declared that he could trust no one else, she did not hesitate to help her brother.

Peter finished college without incident and was in good standing when he graduated. The Whitley Advertising firm hired Peter as a marketing assistant. This corporation was growing rapidly. Supply and demand created a heavy work load, forcing them to hire more help or stay terribly understaffed. Peter found himself extremely busy, forcing him to work harder and longer hours. Most of his assignments were well done, and he was genuinely liked by most of his colleagues. They all worked very hard to meet their deadlines, and with the heavy workload, it didn't take long to develop team camaraderie.

Peter spent some of his free time trying to find a new vehicle. Coming up with enough money to pay the cost of the vehicle in full was next to impossible, so Peter scraped enough funds together for a down payment. Always a practical thinker, Peter passed on the car of his dreams for a car good enough to get him to work and back. This would have to do until he could save a little more money. He rented a home on a winding road overgrown with thick trees. If it weren't such a lovely place, most people would likely not venture down the unlit road out of pure fear of the unknown, but Peter knew the route by heart.

Darkness was creeping into the purple sky. The long, swooping branches of the willow trees that hung over the winding edges of the road seemed to part automatically as his vehicle approached. Coming into view was his huge stone house, which seemed to take over a large area of the skyline. It was old and filled with the character of generations passed. The city's old mayor, Mr. Thompson, had built the magnificent house years ago. Many families occupied this lovely dwelling from its beginning until now. Peter wondered if he was the one who liked it best. No matter who claimed the house as home, the town's people always referred to it as the old Thompson place, a designation that always seemed to fit. The house had a design that would make the average person drool at the chance to own it. Peter loved the large old house. It was cozy and warm inside and marked by a quaintness that enticed visitors to come inside and sit by the oversized fireplace. Peter had rented this old house for two years now and he hoped to someday own it.

Truly Hidden: The Missing Diamonds Mystery

Mrs. Charden was the landlady. Many times Peter approached her to inquire about buying it for himself. Most of the time she would just smile and say it's not for sale. She had a smile that suggested she knew something he didn't and that made Peter wonder what she was thinking. She was such a nice lady and after two years Peter knew she was a person that could be totally trusted. She had the master key to the house and asked Peter if he would like her to bring any packages into the house that were delivered and left outside, especially those that wouldn't fit in the mailbox. Peter was thankful for her help, so when the opportunity presented itself, he would buy her a small bouquet of flowers from the corner flower store. She would smile so big and make such a fuss about how beautiful they were, and that he shouldn't have spent the money for such lovely flowers, but Peter could see beyond the protesting to the look of pure joy in her eyes.

One evening Peter arrived home later than usual. His thoughts lingered on his latest project. As he unlocked the back door, he took a few steps inside and then threw his keys on the table. When his eyes passed over the table, he instantly spotted a long package sitting on the counter. He stood there suspended in time; he knew exactly what it was. For years memories of his visit with his grandfather would drift in and out of his mind but so much time had passed since that visit that it no longer seemed real to him. With the words of his grandfather fully in his mind, he lowered himself onto the kitchen chair in front of the package. His mind journeyed back to his visit and, because he was alone, he allowed a tear to run its course down his cheek. He noticed a letter attached to the top of the package. He removed the taped letter from the box and gently ran his finger along the top of the envelope to open it.

Dear Peter,

As you probably know by reading this letter, your grandfather is no longer with us. I have talked to him often and in great detail about the contents of the package. Here are five of his most treasured items that he instructed me to send to you upon his death. They do not seem to be of any monetary value, but I think they must have meant a great deal to him to insist that I see them given to you after his passing. Your grandfather petitioned me to send these to you immediately after his death and without delay, so I am obediently following his wishes. However, I must warn you that your grandfather's house was ransacked following his death, and I fear the perpetrators may have been looking for the belongings I bequeath to you now. The local authorities are looking into the matter but they have come up with nothing so far. Your grandfather also wanted me to mention the Huntington Museum and a gentleman by the name of Charles Morgan in the letter. These two names mean nothing to me but he insisted that only you and I see the letter in which they were to be written. This wish has been upheld at my end.

Hope this letter finds you well,

Jonathan Stakes, Attorney at Law

"Someone knows," he whispered to himself. His mind began to race. *They must know—or why would they ransack his house? They could only have been looking for the diamonds. Who could it be?* Snapping back to reality, he noticed the door was unlocked. He hurriedly walked over to close the door, turning the dead bolt until he heard it clunk into place. He then turned and stared at the package afraid to open it.

He opened the drawer to remove a small cutting knife. Very gently, he cut the tape that held the wrapping securely in place until the box itself emerged. Removing the top of the box, Peter saw there were five separately wrapped items inside. Reaching in, he took out the first wrapped object and then peeled back the paper to reveal his grandfather's pocket watch—the same watch that Peter's great grandfather had given to his grandfather such a long time ago. It was solid gold and aged with long use and memory. The second hand still made its halting course around the hours, and he wondered if it was his grandfather who had last wound it. The second gift was a small pile of well-worn rosary beads.

Lovingly, he placed them on the table next to the pocket watch. The third item was very small. As he picked up the tissue paper that concealed it, a ring fell back into the box. He placed his index finger into the circle, sliding the ring down the rest of his finger. Lifting it up to his face so he could get a better look at it, he realized it was his grandfather's wedding ring. Peter's eyes moistened as he recognized the intimate memory his grandfather wished to share with him. The fourth gift was a small prayer book. Like the rosary beads, it too looked old and evenly worn, as if the owner had been drawn back to it time and again.

Peter didn't have to guess at what was wrapped in the last package. It was long and narrow. He looked at it for a long time before he reached in to draw it from its snug place in the box. The cane was not heavy, but his heart felt the weight of the moment. Taking a deep breath, he mustered up the strength to unwrap the cane his grandfather had taken such care and precaution to send to him in his final hours. He gently held the cane in one hand, running his other hand along its length until it came to rest on the spot that his grandfather had pointed out to him. This was his grandfather's prized possession, and he had been entrusted with it. The diamonds were his burden now, and he hoped that whoever was searching for them was unaware of their hiding place and their new owner.

One week had quickly gone by and Peter was still uncertain what he should do with the cane and the diamonds. Until he could decide, he hid the box in the highest kitchen cabinet, neatly placing the package behind some canned goods. He wasn't worried about anyone breaking into his house to steal the hidden box, nothing like that had ever happened in the past—and besides, it would take someone with super human strength to get through the oak door that sealed his home. The locks were made of tempered iron and were nearly impossible to pick. There was no doubt in his mind; you would need a key to get in. *And who would brave the windy road, anyway?* he thought to himself as a wry smile flashed across his face.

His confidence would soon be broken. One evening he returned home to find his oak door ajar. He knew instantly that something was drastically wrong. He parked the car and quickly approached the door. The keys still dangled from the lock. His mind began racing. Only his landlady had a set of keys, but she'd never left the door open before. Peter's stomach churned. Cautiously stepping inside the door, he was taken aback by the scene that confronted him. It looked like his house had been taken apart and every bit of it spewed upon the floor. Positioning himself near the door, Peter stood there in shock. He could hear police sirens in the far-off distance, and he suspected that they might be heading in his direction.

When they arrived, they found him, staring blankly at the wreckage.

"Are you Peter Armstrong?" an officer asked him. All Peter could do was nod. The officer took Peter by the arm and asked him if he wanted to sit down before they took him to the station for questioning.

"Why would I have to go to the station?" asked Peter.

Trying to answer his question without causing alarm, the officer replied, "Mrs. Charden has been murdered."

At that moment, it felt like an arrow went right for his heart. The pain the officer's words brought were worse than taking a blow to the stomach. Peter walked over to the only standing kitchen chair and sat down hoping that sitting would ease his pain.

"We just need to ask you a few questions. We know you didn't kill her. A patrol car was stationed at the entrance of the road for the better part of the day, and we know you were at work when she was killed. Peter, do you know why someone would want to kill her?"

Without thinking he said, "No one could get in without the key."

They both turned in unison to stare at the key hanging in the door.

"There was a note left on your kitchen table," Officer Riley stated. Peter reached for the folded piece of paper to read the message, which read: *I know you have them.*

"Do you know what this note is about?" the officer asked.

Peter said he didn't know who could have possibly written it but he knew that whoever had ransacked his grandfather's place likely ransacked his own home and for the same reasons. They knew he had the diamonds.

Tom arrived at his home moments later, having been contacted by the authorities earlier in an effort to contact Peter. Alarmed, he immediately sought Peter at his home. As he entered the house, he surveyed the destruction and noted aloud that, "Someone is after something, but what?"

The police officers finished their questions and promised to be in touch as soon as they acquired further answers. Peter saw them to the door, and then walked over to a chair that had been flipped over on its back. Tom picked up another overturned chair to put back into place. They both started to clean up the mess when Peter remembered the box. His eyes scanned the debris until it rested on the long, cardboard container. Stepping around the debris, he crossed the kitchen and picked up the box, placing it on the table. He scanned the room and noticed the prayer book which lay open and upside down on the floor. He also noticed the gold wedding band sitting on a piece of bread lying on the floor. Placing them both on the table, he calculated what was left. It didn't take long to find the gold pocket watch hiding in the corner next to a cup. It looked like someone had inspected it, saw no value in it, and then threw it against the wall. He found the rosary beads in the box. Nervously, Peter went looking for the cane, which he found broken into two pieces, as if someone had snapped it over their knee. A quick review of the cane eased Peter's mind. They hadn't discovered the diamonds even though they had held them in their hands.

Tom noticed Peter's relief in finding the cane. Concerned, he looked Peter directly in the eye and asked, "What's going on here, Peter? I can see you're in some kind of trouble."

Peter knew he could trust Tom and he truly needed a steadfast friend now, so he shared the whole story with him, including how the diamonds came into his grandfather's possession. Tom stared at Peter in disbelief but quickly became concerned when he realized that whoever had ransacked his friend's home would likely do it again.

"Peter, I think you're in real danger. Do you know what you are going to do? It was pure luck they didn't find the diamonds."

35

They both looked around the room and saw again that almost every inch of the house had been searched.

"You've got to hide those things, Peter. You've got to get them far away from you. If you want, I can help you find a hiding place for one of them, a place where no one would ever think of finding it. My sister Rachel can be trusted, too, and I know she'd be willing to hide one of them, assuming you do not want them both in the same hiding place."

"I really don't want them in the same hiding place. It would be smarter to separate them," Peter replied. "If I were forced against my will to give one up, I wouldn't lose both of them at the same time. Let's think about it a minute. What are the chances of someone coming back here to look for them again?"

"About one-hundred percent," Tom answered quickly, "and when they come back, they'll search the contents of the box with intense scrutiny. Chances are they'd find them."

"Okay. Let's get them out," Peter said as he walked over to the kitchen drawer to grab a knife. Taking the upper half of the cane in hand, he placed it on the table and gently turned it until the repaired spot faced upward. He applied the tip of the knife to the cane and started to turn the knife back and forth on the spot that his grandfather had showed him so many years ago. Memories were flooding his mind as he scraped away the loose wood. He then turned the cane over and tapped the cane into his cupped hand where two precious gems fell into the palm of his hand. They were beautiful. When he saw the size and exquisite beauty of the diamonds, Tom knew the extent of Peter's troubles.

Peter picked out the larger of the two diamonds and handed it to Tom. "This is the one your sister can hide," Peter said apprehensively "I think it's the more valuable of the two stones. It will probably be safer in her possession. I'll keep the smaller one in my keeping. Are you sure you want to involve your sister?"

"Yes. She's trustworthy and, besides, how would anyone know that we had given the diamond to her? Rachel would tell no one, I'm sure of that, and I know you and I won't breathe a word of this to anyone."

"Now where should I hide the other one?" Peter asked aloud. Before he could answer his own question, Peter remembered the letter. He realized that the killer had likely seen the message from the attorney. Peter knew he had to be cautious, especially with his contact through the museum. He would have to hold off contacting Mr. Morgan in case someone was watching him, which means he couldn't sell the diamond right away. And then it occurred to him what his grandfather had done. He had hidden the diamond in plain sight. He laid the tie he wore to work on the table and opened it along the seam with the same knife he used to remove the diamonds from the cane. Taking a piece of duct tape, he placed the crystal clear diamond on the inside of the tie, hoping it would wind up in the knot after he looped it. After trying and retying it several times, he accomplished getting the diamond in the exact place he wanted. No one would ever see it or would ever guess it was there. That way Peter wouldn't worry about it being out of his sight, he could check on it at any time, at least until he could come up with another idea of where to hide it.

CHAPTER FOUR

Concealed Place

Tom went right over to Rachel's house after he called her. She was waiting for him at the front door, wondering what the urgency was. Tom sat across from Rachel at her dining room table. He was trying to focus his thoughts before he started his request. Rachel could tell by the look on Tom's face that he was serious. His usual smile was gone. She waited patiently for him to begin. Her excitement was beginning to build, so she forced herself to sit very still. She didn't want to be a distraction. Tom explained to Rachel the entire situation and that Peter was in need of some rather strange help. Taking his time, he told her every detail. She sat in awe when he dropped the teal diamond into the center of her palm right at the precise moment of the story when Peter had dropped it into his hand. They both sat there looking at it for a great length of time. She smiled as though an idea had flashed across her mind and then looked at Tom and said, "I have a great place in mind for hiding it." She leaned in and whispered her secret in his ear. The smile on Tom's face showed her that he approved of her idea. She asked Tom if he would bring it back in two days because it would take that much time to get everything ready. She had a little preparation to do before the diamond could be hidden safely.

Driving to work the next day was a must because of the rain. The first thing she did after arriving at the design factory was to stop at the office of her employer's secretary to sign a request form to set up a meeting with her employer. The meeting would be later that morning, which gave Rachel some extra time. She went to her locker and then her workstation to do a little clean up before she would leave to get permission. She knocked on the door of her employer's office.

"Come in," said Mr. Trundle. She went in, smiled, and sat down on the chair in front of his desk.

"What can I do for you?" he asked.

"I'm here to ask permission to work on a project of my own. I would like to make a glass fish to put in my living room or maybe to give to my brother for his birthday. I think I could finish it in three or four days if I have the company's approval, and if you'll sign the permission form."

"Of course you can. You haven't worked on any self-projects since you started here and the allotted amount is one personal project a year for each employee, so, yes, I'll sign your permission form for you." He applied his signature to the paper, smiled, and handed it to her.

"Thank you, Mr. Trundle," Rachel said as she got up and left the room.

Taking the form, she folded it and tucked it into her smock pocket. *I might need this later*, she thought. She was already applying her imagination to the new project she was about to begin before she even got back to her work station. The mental picture of the fish was beginning to take form in her mind. It wouldn't be swimming, but jumping—almost straight up out of the water. She would render it with a slight curl to its body as though the fish had broken the surface of the water chasing a bug. She decided that she would apply thick, teal splashes to the piece to give it the impression that water was being thrown in all directions. Getting started was always a challenge for her. It seemed like once she began, however, thought and material would combine and the creation would come to life.

Rachel started with the base of the sculpture. Choosing the right size of rod to begin with was extremely important because it set the tone for the whole project. Rachel reached for a crystal clear glass rod that had a slight tint of blue. She rested it on the edge of the furnace, watching it closely as it took on a red glow in the flame. She rolled the glass as it heated to prevent any dripping or breaking off. When the rod reached a high temperature, she promptly retrieved the hot glass from the fire, and then rested the molten glass in a cup-shaped utensil to form its shape. She then quickly rolled it before it began to cool and thicken.

Walking over to the iron table, she tilted the rod upright with little effort like a seasoned professional and allowed the bottom of it to flatten as it rested on the iron counter, forming the stand on which the fish would rest. Grabbing the glass pliers she pinched off the top part of the melted glass at the stem where it was cooling faster, stepped back to assess her work, and then studied its form until she was satisfied enough to let it cool. Her mind was already racing toward the next day when she would have to inconspicuously get the diamond into the design factory. Her stomach was getting a little queasy and her nerves were already beginning to act up. She hoped she could pull it off without being noticed. Tomorrow couldn't come fast enough.

She got very little sleep that night and, when the hour finally came for her to go to work, her hands shook a little as she entered the design building the next morning. The first challenge was to get the diamond into the building without anyone becoming suspicious. She tried to unhurriedly walk through the security checkpoint, deliberately keeping a casual pace. Rachel calmly walked past the guard station, hoping there would be no delay as she walked through the door to the other side like she did every morning. The only thing different about today was that she was just a little bit quieter. Nothing happened. The guard at the check point simply smiled and wished her a good morning as he always did. She gave him a smile and walked to her locker and then to her work station. The next challenge would be to start the fish.

The average eye could recognize the beginnings of a fish tail, but to the eye of a talented artist like Rachel, a whole world of cause and effect took shape in the raw materials before her. The main part of the fish's body needed to be wrought into shape. This would be the most challenging because this would set the sizing of the fish. Choosing a larger sized glass rod, she placed it on the edge of the open-faced furnace and began to roll it ever so slowly as she moved it deeper into the fire so that the glass would heat evenly. She needed a large piece of glass warmed to just the right temperature if she wanted the fish's body to be proportionately correct. When it grew hot enough, she would have to remove it from the oven and place the diamond.

Surreptitiously she glanced in all directions, making sure she was alone. Once she felt secure in her solitude, Rachel pulled the heated glass from the furnace and then rolled it in an oblong wooden cup until it was ready to be fastened to the tail. She grabbed a set of snipping shears and cut off enough of the rod to form the body before setting her tools down. She gave another quick look to make sure she was still alone before putting her fingers to her mouth to take out the blue diamond that was resting in her mouth. She quickly pushed the diamond into the center of the fish's body, and then just as quickly concealed it in the sculpture. The difficult part was over, and by all outward appearances, she had been successful. By the end of the day, she was looking at a nicely formed fish made out of blue-tinted glass. There was a tremendous amount of detail carved into her creation, which helped conceal the diamond hidden inside. Tomorrow all the extra specifications would be added in order to finish the project.

She glanced at the clock and realized that it was time to go, but paused momentarily, suddenly overcome with doubt. Though she knew the diamond was undetectable, she worried that someone might stop to admire it, drop it, and then discover its secret. What would she do then? *The project is inconspicuous*, she told herself. She left the fish sitting next to projects equally mundane, and then went home.

That night she again couldn't sleep. Her mind lingered on the fish, half-speculating about how she might finish the work and half-anxious that someone had discovered the diamond concealed within it. The next day she hurried to her work station and to her relief, the fish was still there undisturbed. She began by applying the splashes and drips before finishing the fins. The biggest challenge was to form the eyes so the fish would have that cold blank look that only a fish could have. She worked for hours perfecting her sculpture with realistic details that brought the work to life. Just as she finished her work, she heard someone behind her say her name. She turned to see her boss standing there with a look of admiration on his face.

"That is one of the finest pieces of work to come through here in a long time. Is that the project you are working on for your brother?" he asked.

"Yes," she replied with some nervousness.

"Splendid. The craftsmanship is really quite wonderful. Is there any way you could leave this one here and start another one for yourself tomorrow?" The color left her face.

"Oh, Mr. Trundle, I'll be happy to make another one for the company tomorrow if that's alright with you. Because it's the original, this one is special to me. I always find the original to be closer to the imaginative impulse that created it," she replied with a modest smile.

"That would be just fine," said Mr. Trundle with a warm smile. "This one is such an incredible work of art. Do you think you can duplicate another to be so charming?"

"I'm sure that'll be no problem," she replied humbly, "The pattern will be fresh in my mind." Rachel watched his face intently as she answered him.

"Fair enough," Mr. Trundle said with a bit of disappointment in his voice. He was quite taken with the work she had done, and quite likely had hoped to make a gift of it himself." Goodnight, Rachel. See you tomorrow," he said as turned and walked away as abruptly as he had arrived.

Rachel had known Mr. Trundle for a couple of years but never had she been as nervous as she had been this afternoon. She wondered if he had noticed the beads of sweat that had formed on her brow. Realizing the late hour, she quickly picked up the fish and headed for the door before she could be waylaid by other colleagues. She headed for the security gate.

"Your permission form, please," asked Godfrey, the old security guard stationed at the gate. Godfrey had worked the guard station for many years. Everyone knew him as gruff and slightly grouchy. He was one of those people that it was difficult to imagine as a younger person; he seemed as though he had always been old.

"I must have left it in my pocket, I'll go to get it right away," she replied as her hands fumbled helplessly through her pockets.

"Oh, goodness, Missy, I don't know if I have enough time to wait. I have another commitment tonight right after work. I'm sorry but I'm in a bit of a hurry tonight. You'll have to leave your project in the check-out locker tonight."

"Oh, no thank you. I'll hurry," Rachel responded. "I'll be right back," she added as she turned quickly to retrieve the permission slip when Godfrey stopped her again.

"Wait a minute, Missy. Come here." Rachel slowly turned and began to walk back to the counter. He held out his hand and said, "I'll hold the fish for you."

She reluctantly handed him the fish. She had to remain calm, so no one would become suspicious. Forcing herself to walk away, she moved as fast as she could until she was out of sight, and then gradually quickened her pace. She retrieved the permission slip, which she found lying on the work station and then hurried back to the guard station. Her heart sank when Godfrey was nowhere to be found. There was just a note pinned to the board of the guard station, which read: *Sorry, Missy. I had to go. Your fish was safely placed in the check-out locker. You can pick it up tomorrow. Yours truly, Godfrey*

Rachel wanted to cry but there was nothing she could do. She left downtrodden and anxious.

She again slept uneasily, tossing and turning and waiting for the alarm to go off so that she could retrieve the fish. She spent the night and most of the morning chastising herself for forgetting the permission slip. Tears ran the length of her cheek, and she occasionally bemoaned her brother's request, which had caused her such grief and tension. When the alarm finally sounded, she dressed hurriedly and hoped no one noticed the bags under her eyes. She would have to agonize the whole day before she could leave with the fish. This time she would be ready, checking her pocket to make sure her folded permission slip was securely tucked inside. There should be no delay this time. When the work day ended, she headed immediately to the security station to pick up her fish.

"Well hello there, Missy," Godfrey said with a smile on his face not realizing the discomfort his hasty departure the day before had caused her. "Do you have your permission slip? Sorry I had to leave yesterday."

"That's okay," she said politely as she handed him the slip. Godfrey read the slip, turned to the locker behind him, and pulled out the fish. Handing it to her, he asked if it was for sale.

"Not this one," she said, "but I'm working on another one just like it. That one will be coming up for sale. She reached up and put her hand around the throat of the fish and waited until he decided to let it go.

"This fish would look real nice just about anywhere you decided to put it. I'd like to study it for a while but I know I'm keeping you," he said as he smiled politely and then hurried on to the next task.

She drove home with the fish next to her on the seat. It was a nice piece of art but it was just a piece of glass. The attention it was getting was making her uncomfortable. Maybe in her plain apartment it would just blend into the background, as if it had no importance. Arriving home she placed the fish toward the back of her shelving, hoping it would disappear in the clutter of her home décor. She placed it next to a small vase of silk flowers, a couple books, a picture, and a few other items that had collected in her place over the years. She stood back to observe how it disappeared into the background of the room. Apart from the absence of dust, it blended nicely into the room.

The following day Rachel was good to her word. The first project on her list was a new fish for the company. The forming and blowing of the second fish took shape faster than the first one and with considerably less nervousness. The second fish turned out to be just as beautiful as the first one. No one could tell the difference except, of course, the artist who created it in the first place. To the normal eye, the two fish were identical; but to Rachel's eyes, the two fish were asymmetrical, a difference that worried her.

She walked to the counter to turn in the second fish for the company to sell. Her fellow employees complimented her on the well-designed fish and asked if she intended to make another. She replied affirmatively but insisted that she would have to wait a short time so the project would be fresh again. Before she turned to leave she spied a space on the water that was missing a few splashes. Embarrassed at not noticing this before she handed it in, she said, "Oh, no, wait a minute. There's an area that needs to be completed," she stammered as she pointed out the bare spot on the sculpture. "I'll have to finish it tomorrow," she said. Her fellow workers thought it looked perfect but when she pointed out the area that needed work they smiled at her perceptive eye and attention to detail. She took the fish from the counter, turned, and walked back to her workstation. She placed the fish on the table next to her locker. She tapped it on the head and then playfully said, "I'll be back to finish you another time." *It'll be easier to leave this one behind because it doesn't hold a valuable treasure,* she inwardly told herself. She simply left without a backward glance or any reluctance to leave.

CHAPTER FIVE

More Than a Favor

Tom left work at the end of the day. It had gone so well he could have whistled a happy tune, so he grabbed his brief case and began walking toward his car, which he had parked on the street outside of the office building. As he exited the office building, he stopped dead in his tracks. His brief case fell out of his hand to the ground. There were two men rummaging through his car.

"Hey!" hollered Tom. "What are you doing?"

Instantly, their heads popped upright like knobs on springs and they bolted from the car. They ran down the block, looking back only once to observe if they were being followed. Tom let them go. He immediately went to his car. He was shocked by the damage they had inflicted on his vehicle. A window had been shattered. The leather seats had been slit and the stuffing thrown all over the place. The glove compartment was completely emptied of its contents, which had been thrown on the sidewalk. His backseat was sitting on the pavement. The trunk was popped and emptied. Tom instantly called Peter to inform him that his car had been trashed and that someone must know that he was helping him.

"How could they have found out?" Tom asked frantically.

"I don't know," Peter said. "Sit tight and I'll be right there."

Peter couldn't believe his eyes when he pulled up to the curb. He reached for his tie, feeling for the diamond he had hidden in it. As he waited for Peter's arrival, Tom had called the police, who were on the scene when Peter arrived. The two men stepped away from the scene.

"I don't think we should tell the police everything, do you agree, Peter?" Tom whispered. Peter nodded his head in agreement, and then asked Tom if he recognized either of the two men who had ransacked his car.

"No," replied Tom, "not a clue." Tom asked Peter if he knew anyone from his grandfather's past that might know about the diamonds. Peter didn't have to strain his memory too hard before he said he remembered that his grandfather's house had been searched a couple of times, but that the perpetrators never found what they were looking for.

"I think it's becoming obvious that someone knows about the diamonds."

"Well," said Tom, "if someone knows about the diamonds then I think we're in trouble. If they ever catch up to you, you may have to give them the diamond for your life. My car is totaled. Do you think you could pick Rachel up from the train station tomorrow? She will be coming back from a visit with on old friend, and she'll need a ride home."

"I'll be happy to pick her up from the train station," Peter answered without hesitation. He wanted to meet the person who hid the other diamond; and knowing he could trust Tom's judgment, he trusted her too. "How will I recognize her and what time should I be there?"

"Her train will be arriving around ten-thirty in the morning on Saturday," Tom answered. "She has blonde hair and brown eyes, but the easiest way to recognize her is the small red suitcase she carries. It has a little white stripe that makes one complete circle around the whole bag. You can't miss it. She's had it for years and won't part with it. She claims it's just the right size for an overnight bag."

Peter secretly arranged his day in his mind making room for the new task he would be happy to carry out. The train station would be his second stop of the day. The first was a trip to the post office to mail a package. 10:30 approached slowly. Peter was slightly nervous to meet Rachel, and he glanced at his watch repeatedly. After dropping the package off at the post office, he drove to the station, parking his car in the first place he could find. After locking the car door, he slowly walked to the front of the car, glanced around, bent over slightly, and then placed his keys on the top of the vehicle's front wheel. He did this often because he didn't want to carry his heavy keys with him. It was a habit he picked up in college, and it wasn't easily abandoned.

Peter straightened his tie again, grabbed the handle on the door to the station, and easily pulled it wide open. He stepped into the huge antiqued room of the old train station, where the ceilings were extremely high, and people could be seen scurrying everywhere. Many were grabbing their luggage as they raced to catch the train before it began to depart for the next town. He glanced around to survey the different ticketing windows trying to decide which one would give up the information he needed. He then spied a kindly old gentleman, who looked like he had worked there for years. Peter walked up to the uniformed man standing behind the center window and asked where he would find the passengers arriving on the 10:30 train.

"Let me see," replied the elderly man as he glanced at the old, tattered log book which sat on the counter directly in front of him. It appeared to be as old as the ticket agent. Its yellowed pages and bent corners belied years of use and reuse. The man then reached into his shirt pocket, pulling out a pocket watch on a chain. It too looked well-worn by callouses and time. He gently pressed the round knob at the top of the watch. His eyes lit up with a delight when the top sprang open. "That train is running a little late today," he said austerely as he pointed in the direction of the incoming trains. "But you go out that door and down the walk until you come to number twelve. The train will be arriving in about ten minutes."

Peter thanked him and then walked confidently in the direction of the morning trains. When he arrived, a huge engine pulled to a stop. The conductor opened the door and stepped out. He reached down to pull out a small step to place before the door of the train. It took only a few minutes before the passengers began stepping off the train. Peter slowed to a very easy pace and kept his eyes fixed on the exiting passengers to make sure he wouldn't miss Rachel. One person after another exited the train. They would pause for a moment, allowing their eyes to search for a familiar face. Occasionally someone would smile and raise their arm to wave in recognition, and then move on through the crowd.

Before he saw the read bag with the white stripe, Peter knew he was looking at Rachel. He noticed her blonde hair and her big brown eyes. He was taken aback by her beauty. Lost in a daze, he nearly walked headlong into a pole which, as chance would have it, is the moment Rachel recognized Peter. He face flashed red as he sidestepped the pole before stumbling forward in her direction. She held the red suitcase in her right hand and waved to Peter with her left.

Before he could reach her, a man approached her from behind, snatched the red suitcase from her, and then sprinted in the direction from which he had approached. It happened so quickly that Rachel didn't have time to react. Peter reacted immediately, stalking the thief through the crowd. Peter moved deftly through the crowd, grabbing a hold of the man's jacket before throwing him to the ground. Peter held the man firmly by his collar.

"Who are you? What do you want with the bag?" Peter demanded.

"The diamond, man, the diamond," he gasped as he tried to catch his breath.

The response stunned Peter and he let down his guard. Suddenly, the thief elbowed Peter in the chest, knocking the air out of him and causing him to loosen his grip. The thief disappeared into the crowd. Fear settled into the pit of his stomach as he realized that all three of them were in danger. Rising to his feet, he greeted Rachel, who had followed Peter as he had chased the assailant through the crowd.

"You must be Rachel?"

"Yes," she said. "And you must be Peter. Are you all right?"

"Yes. I think so," he said as he handed her the suite case. "I think it would be wise to leave this area as soon as possible."

He walked her toward his car as she reassured him she was unharmed. Her voice soothed his uneasiness.

"Do you know what the man was looking for?" she asked as they walked along.

"I'm afraid I do; he was looking for the diamond."

She stared into his eyes anxiously. Her mind was traveling back to the room where she placed the fish on the cluttered shelf and hoped it was safe in its hiding place. No one knows where it is, she reassured herself. Peter was equally anxious but was smitten with Tom's sister.

They made their way through the station, which was beset with detour signs. The station appeared to be undergoing some remodeling, so pedestrian traffic was guided to a side entrance or so Peter and Rachel thought was the case. Before long the crowd dispersed, and Peter and Rachel found themselves alone in an old, dark part of the station. To their right was an old luggage shoot. They both agreed that they must have taken a wrong turn and turned to head back in the direction that they came from, when a man appeared from around the corner. They approached to ask directions, crossing over the luggage shoot to do so. As they did so, the floor beneath their feet gave way. The chute flew open and gravity pulled them down a long dark shaft, which deposited them on an abandoned basement floor. They hit the floor like a ton of bricks, stunned and hurt. The room was completely black and, before Peter could get his bearings, a large foot was placed across his neck.

"Don't move," a cold voice said in the darkness. One of the thugs grabbed Rachel's jacket and yanked her to her feet. "Empty your pockets," the voice commanded. Her suitcase was emptied and the contents were dumped on the floor. The second thief placed a gun to Peter's head and told him to get up and empty his pockets. Peter gave him the contents and, with his free hand, the gunman examined each article before discarding them down the gutter.

Nothing. We found nothing. It's not here," Peter heard one of them say. Just as quickly as they had arrived, Peter and Rachel found themselves alone in the dark.

"Apparently they didn't find what they were looking for," Peter said sarcastically to Rachel. "Now all we have to do is get out of here, but I'm not sure how. The thugs are gone, so there must be a way."

They could not see how large the room was, what it contained, or how it was laid out. Peter asked Rachel if she was all right.

"Yes," she replied. "How about you?"

"Just a minute and I'll let you know." He adjusted his tie again and then said, "Yes, I'm all right. Take my hand, Rachel."

Rachel gladly took his hand and said, "Peter, I think I have a problem."

He held her hand tighter for a moment and said, "What is it?"

She hesitated a minute and then said, "Well, I'm afraid of spiders."

Peter smiled a smile she did not see. With a twinkle in his eye, he replied, "Don't worry—I'll protect you."

"How are we going to get out of here, Peter?"

"I'm not sure," he answered. "Let's just move ahead very slowly and make our way to the wall so that we can move along it with our hands. Hopefully, we'll find an exit. It sure would make it easier if we had at least a small amount of light so that we could at least see what's directly in front of us."

Hand-in-hand and sliding one foot forward at a time, they began to make their way through the darkness. The first obstruction they faltered into was an old coat rack. They bumped their heads, felt for the hangers, and figured out what it was before they edged their way around it.

"Hey! Let's push this ahead of us so we won't run into anything else," Rachel suggested eagerly, but her idea had to be quickly abandoned. There were too many obstructions—most of which were moldy suitcases that had been strewn all over the place. They were lucky they could move at all as the suitcases formed a maze through which they had to navigate without the use of light.

As their eyes adjusted to the darkness, they could make out the outline of objects in front of them. They became bolder, taking larger steps unaware of the danger that lay at their feet. Their next step sent them catapulting down another old abandoned luggage chute, which fortunately was much shorter than the first. They hit the bottom with a hard thud just as they did the first time. Thankfully, no one was there to search them.

"How many of these old chutes are there?" Peter groaned out loud. Painfully they rose to their feet, but before they got too far, Rachel noted the raised temperature in the room.

"It sure is hot down here."

"No doubt we are a little closer to hell," Peter said wryly. In the darkness they heard a grinding, humming noise, which seemed to be getting louder as they moved along. To Peter it sounded like a compressor. The noise was deafening.

"I see a light on the other side of this room, Peter," Rachel said loudly over the cacophony of sound."

"I do see it," Peter replied loudly, "but I'm afraid to walk across the floor."

"Me too," said Rachel. "But if we don't try to find a way out of here, we'll cook to death."

Peter smiled again and asked Rachel for her hand. This time they would slide their feet a little more carefully to make sure there was a floor in front of them.

"Do you think there are any more luggage chutes on this level?" Rachel asked desperately hoping there wasn't.

"I don't know," Peter answered. "Probably not. We seem to be in some kind of engine room, which is why it's so warm."

Slowly they made their way to the other side of the huge machine room, drawing closer to what little light was coming through a slit next to the small window on a door. Their vision was still hindered by the darkness as they awkwardly walked into an old railing barring a small flight of steps. The railing kept them from falling downward. Through the darkness they could see a stairway leading down another flight of stairs.

"I really don't want to go down there, do you, Peter?"

"No, I don't. Let's see if we can find a different way out. To their left appeared the outline of a large steel door. A small window was set in the center of it. The window had been taped over, so they removed the tape, allowing a splinter of light to enter the room. The more tape they removed, the more light entered the room. They tried the handle…but it was locked.

"Maybe we can find some kind of tool or key to get the door open," Peter suggested.

"In all the old movies the key is sometimes left above the door," Rachel chimed in.

"Well it's a long shot," Peter said as he slid his hand above the doorframe. To his surprise his fingers brushed against a solid object that fell to the floor and disappeared into the darkness. They both fell to their knees to search for the object.

"I think I found something," Rachel said. She lifted the object to the light, revealing an L-shaped implement. "Do you know what this is?" she asked.

"I think it's a cotter key," answered Peter.

"Will it fit in the door?" asked Rachel.

"No," said Peter. "It's not that kind of key, but I don't think this made the sound we heard as it hit the floor. Let's search a little more. Maybe we'll get lucky. "

As Peter moved his foot in search of what he thought was a key, he heard an object scrape across the floor. "Don't move," he said as he bent down in the direction of the sound. His hand searched where he thought the sound had come from and before long he had a key in his hand. Bringing the object to the light, Peter recognized a rusted key that was slightly bent from use. Optimistically, they hoped it might be the key that matched the old corroded door lock. They knowingly glanced at each other as Peter placed the little piece of formed metal into the keyhole. He gently turned the key, trying not to force a turn for fear it would break. Peter applied the right amount of pressure until the key's notches matched the lock's indents—and with a dull screech, the old lock shifted, releasing the latch inside the door. Overjoyed with the thought of escaping their dark prison, they exited quickly, squinting in the sun's glare. They entered a brick-lined courtyard.

"Hey, Peter," Rachel beckoned. "This is some kind of levee. There's nothing but water on the other side. Maybe this is some kind of huge holding tank for the city or a river basin." She turned to walk back to the door where Peter stood holding the door open in case they had not found an exit. "Where do you think we are?"

Before Peter could answer, they heard a horrible barking moving in their direction. Racing around the corner directly at them were two large black guard dogs. Teeth and gums were exposed; and from their throats emanated a low gurgle and growl that sent shivers up Peter's spine. It was obvious there would be no stopping them and, if they stayed where they were, Peter and Rachel were going to be torn to pieces. They very quickly edged themselves back into the darkness. Peter could feel the dogs throwing themselves against the door as he closed it behind him.

"I don't think we can get out this way," Rachel sighed. "That was too close." She was still shaking. "What are we going to do now, Peter?" she asked.

"We definitely do not want to go out there again," Peter replied. Suddenly the staircase seemed like a good alternative. Peter held her by the hand and took the first step down and then another. The steps seem to be strong enough to hold his weight, so she followed. One step after another until one of the abandoned steps would take no more and collapsed under her feet. Her shoe fell off her foot and the sound lingered before it finally hit bottom. Peter reached for her with lightning speed and hung on to her with the power of a vice grip before she could fall through. He grabbed her arm hard enough to cause a bruise—and he knew if he didn't hang on tightly enough, she would fall. She clenched on to Peter's arm with equal fear. Quickly he lifted her from the rotten trap, and as he pulled her toward himself he could feel another partially rotten board begin to give out under his own foot. *These steps will never support our weight,* he thought, *we'll have to descend faster or the steps will crack beneath our feet.* Peter took the lead and pulled her along fast until they were safely standing below on the cement landing facing a huge wooden door, which now was their only escape.

"Are you okay?" Peter asked her.

"Yes," she replied. "Thanks to you." Rachel was not going to just hold Peter's hand. Shaking, she hung onto his arm like she would never let go. She was truly scared and not willing to let up on her grip. Peter straightened his tie, put his hand on top of hers, and liked the fact that she was tightly hanging on to him.

Peter tried the door. It loudly creaked as the hinges were forced to slide past each other. They both strained to see out the slight opening as the door was pulled forward. It looked like an abandoned subway, with rusted old tracks laying where they had been used years ago and the huge cavity of a building. It had the look of being abandoned and the smell of mildew lingered in mid-air, assaulting any nostril that would dare enter the interior of the neglected building. They stood there in complete indecision. They were afraid to be too daring.

"Should we step out?" asked Rachel. "I think we could try, I don't see any dogs."

Peter replied, "They must be on an upper level."

"Let's not go too far from the door until we are sure there are no dogs out there," suggested Rachel.

"Just a minute," said Peter as he bent down to pick up an old brick that was lying close to the building. He wedged it between the door and its frame so it wouldn't lock behind them. They took several steps and then stopped to listen for the sounds of encroaching danger. They heard nothing, so they took several more steps. This time a heart-thumping noise like the sound of an engine suddenly penetrated the room. They turned in unison and raced back behind the door. After waiting a few minutes, and breathing a deep sigh, they realized that the noise posed them no danger.

"Let's try again," said Peter.

Slowly stepping back out, they walked with a little more confidence. Looking in both directions and seeing nothing, they had to choose which way to go. At least there was some light coming from high in the rafters. They thought that maybe it was some sort of skylight but it was hard to figure out exactly where it was coming from. Before they started walking any further, Peter looked for anything that could substitute for a shoe. He spotted a small book lying on the ground, picked it up, and then looked for rope of some kind to fasten the book to Rachel's bare foot. Straightening his tie, he knew he couldn't use it as rope; it was too important doing the job it was doing.

"Let's walk a little bit to see what we can find," Peter suggested.

They were in a huge area, and the ceiling was so high that if they looked up it appeared that the building was swaying. Neither of them were prone to vertigo, so they assumed that the light streaking through the ceiling must be playing tricks on them and dismissed any thought of danger. Hanging out of the wall was a long thin cable. Peter spotted it and instantly thought it would make a good rope substitute. He walked over to the wire, grabbed hold of it, and then began tugging at it. The cable didn't want to give up, so Peter wrapped one loop around his hand to get a better grasp and then pulled harder until the wire finally came free of the wall. Peter then asked Rachel to put her foot on the book, which he placed on his knee. She obliged, and he tied the wire around the book and her foot until it became a makeshift shoe.

"Try walking on that to see if it works," he said.

She took a few steps, turned, and walked back in his direction, smiling in appreciation as she did so. Suddenly her face lost its color as her eyes wandered from Peter's eyes to the space to the left of his head. Peter slowly turned to see what caused her discomfort, and his eyes were quickly drawn to a small hole in the wall from which the rope had been pulled. From the hole trickled a small stream of water that appeared to be gathering force the longer they watched.

They took several steps backward to avoid getting wet. The hole was getting larger by the moment as the flow of water increased at a rapid speed. Peter grabbed Rachel's hand anxiously and started pulling her along, trying to get the both of them as far from the wall as fast as he could. As they hurried away from the wall, Rachel could see the water increasing in volume in her peripheral vision. She ran as fast as her homemade shoe would allow her to do. Suddenly the wall gave way, and the slow, steady stream that piqued their fear had turned into a surge of water rushing from the gaping hole in the wall. The room quickly filled with water and was already nipping at their heels. The little book

Rachel was wearing as a shoe was wet and sloshing, and she could feel it tearing apart. The water was rising, and before long, they were both slogging through water up to their ankles.

"I can see a staircase!" yelled Rachel.

Peter too had seen the staircase and instinctively headed in that direction knowing this might be their only way out. The water level had risen past their knees and continued to rise as water filled the room. The closer they got to the stairway the harder it became to gain any distance as the water had climbed above their waists, slowing their progress considerably. When they finally reached the staircase, they quickly climbed the steps two at time until they reached a level that freed them from the water. They paused momentarily to assess their situation, wary of the water's rapid climb up the staircase. Looking up they noticed that the staircase hugged the wall and wound up to a landing near the ceiling.

"There must be two hundred steps," Rachel sighed.

They moved quickly up the staircase as the water continued to fill the room. The higher they went, the heavier their feet became. They were exhausted, gasping for air; it took nearly all of their energy and effort to ascend each step. Suddenly, the ceiling above them came alive as hundreds of bats disturbed by the rising water and their own frantic movement up the staircase swooped down out of the rafters. They flew swiftly by Peter and Rachel, encircling the both them momentarily as they rushed madly toward an opening in the ceiling.

"Follow the bats!" Peter yelled.

As they scaled the remaining steps, they observed the bats escape the rising water through a window in a door at the far end of the landing; however, when Peter and Rachel reached the door at the top of the staircase, they discovered that the door was locked. Peter grabbed hold of the doorknob and tried to push down the door, hoping that the force of his body would release the door lock, but the door wouldn't budge.

"Now what are we going to do?" asked Rachel in a panic.

"I don't know," Peter answered equally frustrated and anxious as the water continued to claim more and more of the staircase. The window through which the bats had escaped appeared big enough for Rachel to pass through. Turning to one another simultaneously, they both came to the same conclusion at the same time.

"Why don't you boost me up there, so that we can see what's on the other side?" Rachel suggested. Peter cupped his hands on his knee, and she placed her hands on his shoulders as he lifted her up to the window. When she was high enough she placed her left hand on the frame of the window so that she could pull herself upward. She then lifted the window high enough to get her head through so she could get a clear view of the room on the other side of the door. The room was more well-lit than the one they were in, and she noticed that there were suitcases piled high and vacant animal cages strewn all over the room. The bats had passed through another window that opened to the outside world.

"If we can find a way to get through to the other side, we might find a way back to the main station," she reported back. With Peter's help, she shimmied through the window, contorting her body until she was able to pass her legs through the window, and then land safely on the floor on the other side of the door. As her feet hit the floor, the water breached the edge of the landing, causing Peter to frantically try the door again. But the door remained locked and rusted in place.

Rachel too tried the door but found it locked. She quickly searched the area for the key but came up empty. Peter could hear her rustling about in the other room.

"What's the matter?" Peter asked. "Peter, I cannot open the door!" she yelled back to him in a panic. "And I cannot find the key!"

"The door is old. Find something to smash the door knob with. Perhaps the lock will give way once the knob is broken."

She found a loose brick in the far corner of the room beneath the open window, picked it up, and started to pound the door knob. With encouragement from Peter, she pounded the door knob again and again with the brick—each blow harder than the last. Her last blow sent the rusted door knob flying to the floor, signaling Peter to again try the door. Peter put his shoulder to the door, leaned back, and then suddenly launched his weight forward, applying all of his force to the door, which flew open. The suddenness with which the door gave way caused Peter to stumble through the doorsill to the floor. When he gathered himself, he saw Rachel standing over him, relieved to have Peter close to her again. Looking back over the landing, they noticed that the water had slowed its pace. Nevertheless, they were relieved to be free of the darkness.

The room they now stood in looked like it had been used more recently. There was luggage scattered everywhere. Some of the luggage looked as if it had been there a hundred years and some of the luggage looked like it had been left there yesterday. They noticed a door across the room and headed in that direction when Rachel stopped suddenly in her tracks.

"Hey look," she said. "There's my old suitcase."

"Are you sure this one is yours?" asked Peter.

Rachel picked up the suitcase and lifted the little latch that held the case closed. She reached inside the bag and pulled out a pair of leather-bottomed slippers, which she immediately put on her wet, sore feet.

"This is definitely my bag," she said, befuddled as to how it came to be here in this room.

Suddenly the door to which they were heading flew open with great force and with a loud bang. A uniformed man stepped inside the door. He appeared to be looking for specific luggage but was shocked to find himself face-to-face with Peter and Rachel, who were equally shocked by the uniformed man's sudden appearance. The guard regained his composure and remembered his professional authority.

"This room is off limits to anyone but station personal," he barked. "What do you think you two are doing in here? How did you get into Lost and Found? This is a locked quarter and trespassers are subject to fines."

Peter and Rachel were speechless and couldn't find the words to explain how they had come to be in Lost and Found. Their silence was understood as obstinacy by the uniformed man, who went red in the face as though he were about to explode. In proportion to what had occurred earlier that day, the anger of this little man didn't scare them one bit. They were just happy to be safe from the caverns below.

"Alright follow me," he demanded, "You'll have to go to the detention center to be questioned. " You'll probably be fined," he impatiently warned.

Peter and Rachel simply smiled at one another, relieved that their ordeal was almost over.

Obediently, they followed the station officer. In the distance they could here sirens sounding likely as a result of the water leak below. As they entered the main lobby of the station, they saw numerous fire engines and police cars stationed outside and several fire and police men rushing about the building.

"Hey, hold up there!" a firemen yelled in their direction as he walked up to them to inquire if they knew anything about the cause of the flooding in the basement of the station.

The station officer said he didn't know anything, which forced Rachel and Peter to hold back a smile. When the fire chief turned to look at the two of them, Peter and Rachel just shrugged their shoulders. They had to act dumb or be held for hours of endless questioning that would prove nothing. The station officer repeated the command for them to follow him as he turned and walked toward the train station. Peter and Rachel began to follow him, but with all the excitement, they hesitated before they moved. They noticed that the station officer walked off without making sure they were following and, so, Rachel and Peter took the opportunity to evade him. They quickly moved in the opposite direction. Leery of everyone they passed, they steadily walked through the station, trying not to draw any attention to them. They had not gotten far when someone yelled for them to stop. Fear gripped them as they both turned in unison to see who was calling.

It was a police officer.

"What's going on here?" he said to them. "Do you two know anything about what's going on out there?"

Calmly, Peter explained that he had picked Rachel up from the train and that they were just leaving.

"When did that train come in?" the officer asked impatiently.

"Ten-thirty," Peter replied.

"Ten-thirty!" the officer shouted. "What have you been doing all day?"

Rachel hugged Peter's arm, smiled at the officer, and politely said, "Why, we've been doing a little walking."

Her sweet smile disarmed the officer's suspicion, and he motioned for them to move along. She smiled again, took Peter by the arm, and the two of them started to meandered away from the officer, who watched them as they walked away. Rachel knew she had persuaded the officer into letting them leave but what she didn't know was that Peter too had been persuaded. He loved the feel of her hand in his arm.

Their destination was Peter's car. All they wanted to do was get away from the station area and any diamond-hunting criminals. As they were walking back to the parking lot, Rachel remembered Peter had to empty his pockets and the contents were thrown down the drain, so she asked Peter how he would start his car. Peter smiled at Rachel as he remembered his hiding place.

"Don't be critical of me," Peter said. "I've been doing this since college, and it has always worked for me."

She looked at him with a puzzled expression until Peter reached under the front wheel of his car and retrieved a chain full of keys that patiently sat on the tire like a robin nesting on its eggs. This time Peter was pleased with his almost careless habit because all the contents of his pockets were at the bottom of some drain system but his car keys were in his hand.

The drive to Rachel's was uneventful. They were tired and seemed to be unwinding from the seemingly disastrous day. The conversation flowed like sweet perfume from flowers. He loved to hear her laugh as they talked. She directed him to where she lived. It was getting late, and the dark night seemed to penetrate all tranquil existence. As they drove up her driveway, it took only moments for Rachel to perceive that something was terribly wrong and stopped talking immediately. This made Peter instantly look her way to see the expression on her face. Her worried stare was directed toward her house, so he turned in that direction to see what she was intently staring at. The lights were on and the window was smashed. The door was open and a look of disarray spewed from the building. Chills penetrated her very being as she realized her house had been broken into. They slowly walked up to the open door of the house cautiously in case someone dangerous was lingering inside.

It was obvious the house had been searched. The reason for the break in hit their thought like a bee zooming in for the kill. Rachel forced herself to go through the door knowing the first thing she had to check was the glass fish. The whole room was thrown into total disarray. Her eyes shot to the shelf where the fish should have been, but there was just an empty space. She fully realized the value of the fish, and her heart sank when she thought it could be missing. Instantly she began scanning the floor for the missing fish, identifying other treasured belongings as her eyes raced across the spewed possessions. She lost hope by the minute. As she continued her search she caught a small glimpse of glass protruding slightly from under a couch cushion that had been casually thrown to the corner of the room. She slowly lifted the cushion to expose the slightly damaged fish. Rachel slowly bent down to retrieve her precious creation, hoping its damage hadn't given away its deeply hidden secret. With one glance of her artist's eye, she could see it was indeed intact, with only a few drops of water missing from the ocean stand, and a repairable gouge from its side.

Peter stood there just watching her, unable to move. His mind seemed to be playing a repeat scene from the past. Unable to believe what he was seeing, a new kind of uneasiness was beginning to take hold of him. He and Tom had taken an awful chance, and now it has come home to haunt them like a never-ending fear. They had placed Rachel in an extreme amount of

71

danger. With this playing in his head, he could not stop starring at her. He would die if anything happened to her.

Rachel walked to the shelf and placed the fish in its place. It looked funny being the only object on the bookshelf. Turning to ask Peter for help with some of her larger pieces of furniture, she saw a strange look on his face which made her uneasy. She could tell that Peter's mind was turning over deeply disturbing thoughts. She could see it in his eyes. Physically he was there, but mentally he was not.

"What's the matter?" she asked.

Her voice snapped him out of his stupor, and he looked her right in the eye. He didn't want to scare her anymore then she already was.

"Here, let me help you put things in their place," he said trying to hide how troubled he really was.

They worked until the early hours of the morning. Daylight was beginning to peek over the top of the horizon, sending its soft rays of filtered sunshine through the treetops. At last her apartment was beginning to look acceptable again, hiding traces of the battle her home had endured. The furniture was upright and back in its resting spots. There were many broken items that were placed in an old box, patiently awaiting their decision to be kept for repair or to be discarded. Rachel felt some sadness about losing a few treasured items. Some of them were full of memories from long ago, but she didn't let on to Peter. The look on his face was disturbing enough.

"Would you like some coffee?" Rachel offered Peter, hoping it would ease his mind.

"I would love some," Peter replied. The coffee tasted so good, and it was a boost to his aching body. They each sank into a comfortable chair to sip the coffee.

"Where is it?" Peter asked, although he was afraid of the response he would get. "Did they get the diamond?"

Rachel responded by first looking intently into Peter's eyes before walking his gaze to the glass fish on the shelf with her gaze.

"You mean it's in there?" Peter asked quizzically.

She nodded her head in affirmation. Peter leaned back in the chair and breathed a deep sigh of relief.

"You hid it in a good place. I never would have guessed it was there," he said. And then it dawned on him that whoever was searching for the diamond never guessed it either. Now it was time for Peter to confide in Rachel. He waited until she looked him in the eye, and then he applied his thumb to the diamond hidden in his neck-tie and pushed until the diamond protruded out.

She reached up and felt the round stone hidden within the cloth. "You're not going to leave it there all the time, are you?"

"No," replied Peter, "but it's the best place I can think of for now."

"Rachel, you can't stay here by yourself; it's too dangerous."

"I know," she agreed. "I'll talk to Tom today to see if we can come up with something. Maybe he'll stay with me during the week, and I can go home on the weekends."

"That would be the best."

Peter knew it was getting closer to the time he would have to leave. There were two reasons he was finding this very difficult. Seeing her house so terribly ransacked made him concerned for her safety. The second reason was that he had become very attached to her in the short period of time they had spent together. Becoming very serious, he began to approach a delicate subject without knowing if Rachel's feelings were the same as his.

"Rachel, if you are going to be home next weekend, would you consider having dinner with me?"

Her big brown eyes rested softly on his face. She smiled at him warmly, remembering the day and how she held his hand when she was scared. His question brought his handsomeness into focus for her and gave her own feelings clarity.

"I would enjoy that very much, Peter."

"Wonderful. I am sorry our first meeting has come under such trying circumstances though the day wasn't without its fun," he said wryly. "Would you mind giving me your phone number? I'll give you a call before evening to find out if you and Tom have decided on a plan and to confirm dinner arrangements."

He moved toward the door to leave. Rachel was a little sad he was leaving. She walked him to the door. He waited for her to write her phone number down before she handed him the small slip of paper. Standing there she looked up at him and thanked him for his help. She smiled shyly and then said, "I think you did me more of a favor than you thought you would be doing today."

He couldn't stop looking into those big brown eyes. As if there was a magnetic pull, he leaned down and gently kissed her, placing one hand gently around her waist. She was surprised and delighted, and almost swooned with the kiss.

"I better be going. We both need to get some rest," he said as he again gestured toward the door.

Peter arrived home that morning and fell right into bed. Sleep over took him like a drug. He slept soundly until a ringing phone woke him from his slumber. By the time he grabbed the phone, there was only a dial tone on the other end. He slammed the phone back into its cradle before drifting off back to sleep. But the phone rang again, waking him again. His agitation motivated him to the phone, which picked up in agitation and said, "Hello?"

"Am I speaking to Peter Armstrong?" a male voice said methodically.

Peter replied affirmatively.

"Please, allow me to explain the situation. My name is Charles Morgan. Your grandfather and I have been close friends for a good number of years. He has contacted me on a number of occasions. We have had many discussions about the situation involving you and your inherited treasure. I'm wondering if you and I could arrange for a meeting to discuss any problems you may be having in regards to your inheritance."

"I was going to contact you in the near future," Peter replied, "to discuss the transaction concerning my grandfather's intentions. Yes, an arranged meeting would be best, I think. I was purposely holding off on contacting you at the museum. Apparently there has been a leak in my grandfather's plans. I can't say there hasn't been some difficulty. I am being followed. The secret must have leaked out and someone has been persistent in his or her search for my inheritance. I couldn't take a chance in contacting you as I fear my every move is being watched. Now there is too much at stake for me not to be cautious. Let's arrange a time and place to meet, but we must be very guarded."

Peter thought this man could be trusted and that he could shed some light on his grandfather's intentions. He longed to hear anything about his grandfather.

"Will you be free to meet at one-thirty Tuesday afternoon?"

"Yes. That'll be fine. Where would you like to meet? We need to choose an inconspicuous place with little foot traffic."

"I believe we could meet at the Old Clock Tower Café. Are you familiar with the restaurant?" Mr. Morgan asked.

"Yes. It's just past the old downtown area," Peter replied. "It's west of the wharf. I'll be there."

"Good," said Mr. Morgan. "Tuesday at one-thirty. I'll see you then."

CHAPTER SIX

The Dangerous Fix

Rachel was studying the fish sitting on the shelf behind the flower arrangement. She realized that it would have to take it back to the factory to fix the broken splashes that were purposely put there to conceal the diamond inside. To the average eye the treasure inside would not be detected. The splashes were placed there just as a precaution. It wouldn't take much time and effort, but it would have to be done.

The next morning, while having coffee with Tom, Rachel reminded him that she might be an hour or two late coming home from work that evening because she would be repairing the fish after work. After coffee, Tom dropped her off at her car, and she drove to work. She went directly to Mr. Trundle's office to ask for a permission slip to again bring the fish back into the glass blowing area and retouch the broken areas.

"What happened to that prize-winning fish that everyone admired?" Mr. Trundle asked inquisitively.

"The fish fell off its shelf at home and some of the finer details broke. It just needs a quick reworking."

"What a shame. Well, feel free to use the shop, but remember the new apprentices are in training every day this week. You may find it difficult to find space enough to get your work done, let alone touch your fish. Feel free to work after hours if you need to. Just make sure you follow company policy."

"Thank you Mr. Trundle. It shouldn't take long. After hours will be just fine."

She left the fish safely wrapped in a towel and then placed the glass fish into a small brown case designed for transporting ceramic and glass work. She kept the case next to her station until she was ready to remove the damaged creation and begin the repair. Ten minutes before closing time, the noise level in the building began to increase as her fellow workers cleaned up their workstations and made their way home. She could hear the hum of their chattering as exited the building. Moments later the building was completely silent.

The silence made Rachel uncomfortable, which was surprising because she was no stranger to working in the building after hours. Maybe it was the rumble of thunder she could hear in the distance growing louder in anticipation of the approaching storm and the faint drops of rain drumming the windows. Perhaps, and more likely, it was the intrusion into her home and the danger posed by recent events.

"This is silly," she said to herself aloud.

She assured herself that she would be fine. The guard remained just feet away and would be there throughout the evening. The sun still shown through the office windows, assuring her that she was secularly alone, so she slowly unwrapped the fish and brought it out into the open, gently setting it on the rotating work platform. She studied the areas that needed repair and began replacing the glass pieces where she intuitively knew they should go. She worked the glass fish until she was satisfied with the repairs. She was so focused on her work, however, that she failed to notice the waning light and the late hour. When she finished her work, she stepped back to admire her work but when she did so she caught a glance at the clock. An hour and a half had passed, and she was alone in a dimly lit building.

She instantly began to put her things away when she heard a noise from across the room. Sitting very still she trained her ears in the direction of the noise but heard nothing. Taking the fish in hand, she quickly wrapped it in cloth. Before she could finish wrapping the glass fish, she heard the noise again. Wasting no time, she quickly put the wrapped fish in the small soft case and glanced around the room. She moved quickly to shut down her station when again she heard a noise in the distance. This time she thought the noise to be steps, heading in her direction. Her heart beat faster. She reached for her jacket, shut the lights off at her workstation, and moved swiftly to the tall cabinet next to her work station to hide. The storm outside cast lightning, which periodically threw flashes of light across the night sky, illuminating the room. Once inside the cabinet, she pushed slowly to open the door just enough to see through the crack. Should stood still, holding her breath but her body began shaking out of fear. Though difficult, she heard the sound of approaching footsteps.

Momentarily, she thought she could hear whispering, so she listened intently for the sound of a familiar voice in hopes that it was just a co-worker returning late for an item that they had left behind. Over the sound of her beating heart, she heard someone whisper, "Do you think she's still here?"

Without warning the lights went on, and she began to feel like a rabbit caught in a trap. Her eye desperately peered through the crack in the cabinet door, searching for the intruders. She was terrified, and her breath quickened. Her heart started pounding more loudly than before, and she was sure it would give her whereabouts away. Suddenly, two men appeared in her view. There were two of the worst looking characters she had ever seen—unclean, unshaven, and looking like they were capable of caring out any awful threat that was made. The hair on the back of her neck stood on end.

"Oh, God, please help me," she whispered quietly to herself.

At that very moment Tom wondered where Rachel was, forcing him to remember the conversation that took place that very morning. She said she would be late tonight. Looking at the clock on the wall he realized that she was two-and-a-half-hours late, which made him uneasy. He immediately called Peter in a panic. Given the circumstances, they agreed that the best course of action was for Tom to drive to her place of work as soon as possible. Peter insisted that he would meet him there as soon as he could.

As Peter was driving as fast as he could to the Design Center, a feeling in the pit of his stomach was becoming stronger.

He couldn't stop his foot from applying more pressure to the accelerator, even though common sense screamed at him to slow down in the pouring rain.

Tom hurriedly got into his car and started racing to the Glass Design building. His only thoughts were on Rachel, and he gave little concern to the dangerous conditions created by the torrential downpour, which was punctuated by thunder and lightning. His was acutely worried about Rachel, so he didn't realize that his foot increased pressure on the accelerator, causing the car to move forward faster and faster, leaving wisdom far behind. Visibility was low, and because of the static interference created by the lightning storm, he didn't have his car radio on, so he was unaware of the possible flood conditions on the roads ahead. In his hasty determination, he took the most direct route, hoping to get to Rachel as soon as possible.

Without warning his car began to hydroplane across the road for several feet before inertia took over and the car came to rest on the surface of the water. The flood waters had claimed the road, expanding in all directions to form a small pond upon which he was suddenly adrift. His car acted like a boat, floating down the road for a short time before it came to a rest. The flood waters began breaking against the side of the car, and it didn't take long for the water to kill the engine, rendering the steering wheel useless. Because of his lack of caution, he was caught off guard and was totally surprised by the waterline that ran across the road he was traveling.

The car felt as though it had become lodged securely against other debris, and he felt as though he wouldn't be swept away by the surging waters. As he struggled to free himself form the car and to plan his next course of action, he thought he heard someone cry for help. He opened his eyes wide to better see in the dark. The lightning helped him see a short distance in front of him, and he scanned the water until he spotted someone sitting on the top of a turned over truck that was tipped on its side. The flood waters had nearly submerged the vehicle.

Like Tom, Kayleigh was also driving unaware of the small, newly formed lake that had laid claim to the road. When she came over the small incline, she thought that the road would be as it always was when she often traveled it. Applying the brakes as she went over the top of the hill did nothing to stop her decent to the other side. It was too dark. She never saw the water until it was too late. She lost control of her vehicle much as Tom had done. Her truck turned over in the rushing waters and came to rest along the edge of the forest where the water began to submerge her vehicle. Kayleigh managed to pull herself out the window to the top of her truck. She was trapped, she was cold, and the water all around was rising at a rapid rate. She had no choice but to stay put and wait for the time when she would have to swim for her life.

Tom remembered the flashlight he kept under his seat, knowing it would come in handy one day. He hoped the batteries were still able to generate enough energy to throw a beam of much-needed light. Reaching under the seat, he grabbed the flashlight, the first aid kit, a folded blanket, and nylon rope. Not knowing how long his car would stay afloat, he was trying to figure out a way to help her. Pushing the button to see if the flashlight would go on, he was surprised to see a beam throw itself in the opposite direction. Scanning the top of the water, the ray sliced through the darkness coming to rest on the turned truck and its wet female passenger.

"Stay right there!" Tom yelled to her. "When I drift a little closer, I'll throw you the end of a rope. Are you all right?" he asked her.

"Yes. I'm all right," she replied. "Just very cold."

Tom tied a knot in the end of the rope and yelled for her to try and catch the end as he began to throw it as hard as he could in her direction. Tom tried twice unsuccessfully. The third time he yelled, "Here it comes!"

She responded by grabbing the rope. But her hand could not keep hold. She hadn't realized how cold her fingers were because her hand couldn't maintain the grip. You'll have to try again!" she yelled. "My hands are too cold. They're not doing what I want them to do."

"I'll throw it farther if I can," he responded calmly, realizing that she was beginning to panic. "Wrap it around your waist this time."

He tossed the rope with as much momentum as he could muster. The rope flew higher and further than it did before, and Kayleigh reached out as far as she could. She managed to grab the rope again but her hands remained too weak for surety. She wrapped the rope around her waist, using her body as an anchor for the rope, which enabled her to maintain a more secure grip.

"I've got it!" she yelled back to Tom.

"Good!" Tom said reassuringly. "Now, pull slowly."

She lowered herself into the frigid waters, and collectively they pulled her toward Tom's car. When she was close enough, Tom asked her to take his hand as he helped her climb in the window of his car. He could see she was shivering, so he grabbed the blanket to help her fight off the chill.

"Thank you so much. I am so cold, and your car is still a little warm. My name is Kayleigh Daniels and I'm so thankful for your help. "

Tom couldn't help but notice her beauty. Her long, dark hair was wet, and her big, dark beautiful eyes couldn't hide the fear behind them but they still sparkled. His admiration was momentary, however. The danger that he was currently in and the danger that Rachel might be in came rushing to the forefront of his mind. He conveyed his concern for his sister to Kayleigh, who offered to help him if she was able. The two of them put their minds to getting out of their current predicament.

"The water is deep," he cautioned.

"We could swim to the other side," Kayleigh suggested, "but then what?"

"I need the car to work," Tom said to no one but himself.

Just as he was beginning to formulate a plan, the unexpected happened. A mile upstream a levee, which had been overrun by the rain, collapsed, sending a torrent of water downstream in their direction. The speed and depth of the water changed almost instantaneously. The new flood surge pulled the car from its moorings, floating it down the flood waters.

The car whirled directionless down the waters for several yards before slamming into an old stone wall along the road. Kayleigh was ruthlessly thrown to the other side of the car seat. She grabbed at anything to hold on to brace herself for impact. Tom too went along for the wild ride, but the force of the deluge flung him over the top of the stone wall when the car struck it. He was abruptly deposited him in the grass on the other side of the wall. The impact almost killed him. He just laid there unconscious.

When he came to, his wrist radiated pain, but he noticed that the flood waters had receded. The torrent of rushing water must have cleared whatever barrier was holding the flood waters here on the road. In her effort to help, Kayleigh jumped out of the car but landed in the mud. The mud sent her sliding down the small hill. Her feet didn't even hit the ground or so it seemed. Once she managed to stop her slide, she managed to crawl back over to Tom, who looked dazed by the experience. Touching his cheek, she asked him if he was alright.

"I think I'm fine," he said, but there was a stabbing pain in his head. He raised his hand to rub his forehead as if that small gesture would ease the pain, "Can you help me up?" he asked Kayleigh.

In response she tried to stand upright in the mud, pulling him up by the arm once she had firmly planted her feet. The rope he had used to rescue Kayleigh was still wrapped tightly around his arm and was cutting off the circulation and causing his arm to turn blue. The rope proved difficult to remove, having tightened in the water, and she could tell that Tom was in a good deal of pain. She quickly went back to the car where Tom said he believed that there was a knife in the glove compartment. She retrieved the knife, which she found lying where Tom had said it would be. The knife was just a pocket knife. The blade was small and dull and no match for nylon rope, but she worked diligently, sawing at the rope until it fell from Tom's arm. Relief flashed across his face as he began rubbing the arm gently to help the blood circulate in his arm.

They were both cold—even Tom was shivering by this time. He again wrapped Kayleigh in the damp blanket lying in the car. To their good fortune the car had been pushed up on the side of the road along the rock wall. With the waters receding, it was free of any debris but Tom held out little hope that the engine would ever turn over. Nevertheless, he tried it, and the engine nearly ignited.

"Almost got it," he said out loud.

"Try it again," Kayleigh encouraged, and, so, Tom turned the key one more time. To their surprise the car turned over.

"I'll let it run for a while," Tom said. He was hopeful that the car would remain running.

After five or ten minutes they were again surprised when Tom pushed a button on the dashboard and warm air began to push its way out the vents to penetrate the car's interior. Kayleigh wanted to purr like a kitten with delight; it felt so good. Tom's arm was beginning to gain circulation. He was still very wet and still extremely cold, but this warming air was beginning to help.

"Now's the big test to see if it's a truly good car," Tom said softly. He moved the gear into drive and the navy blue Mustang began to move forward slowly. Without stopping he let the high idle take him forward in the direction of the road. Not wanting to test his luck by going uphill, he let the car idle down a slight incline, which would eventually lead onto the road. He was thankful there wasn't a curb. He feared the bump would kill the engine. As soon as they were on the road, his thoughts bounced back to the situation that brought him there in the first place, Rachel. He knew he had to make his way to the Glass Design factory without delay, and turned to ask Kayleigh's permission to go to the Design Center first.

"I understand," Kayleigh said. "You better head right to the place where she's supposed to be. I'll ride along and try to warm up along the way." The heat was now blowing out very warm air, and even Tom was beginning to feel comfortable.

Wanting to push the accelerator to the floor was a natural reaction for Tom, but he remembered the lesson the rain had just taught him. He elected to drive more cautious. Carelessness would just slow them down. Keeping his speed in check was difficult because anxiety was driving him forward. Keeping his thoughts in check was disturbing because they were completely directed toward Rachel as he made a steady path to where she was.

CHAPTER SEVEN

In Time

Rachel stood frozen inside the cabinet, watching every move the two men made and waiting to see where their evil minds would direct their next move. She could hear every word they spoke.

The words slavered out of the first perpetrator's mouth, "Maybe the broad's not here. And if she's not here, how can we tell where her work station is?"

"Look, quit talking. All we have to do is nab her and we get the diamonds. It's an even trade."

Rachel could see his ugly smile through the slit in the cabinet door. The realization that they knew that she had the diamond made her stomach churn. How they knew remained a mystery. They began carelessly searching the larger cabinets and in every crevice large enough to hide a human being. As their probing got dangerously close, her heart began to pound harder. She held her breath.

"Hey, lookie here, Skid," one of them said to the other as he reached for the second diamond-less fish sitting at the back of the table at her station. "I think I like this one, so I'm just going to take it.

"Oh, what do you want that for?" Skid replied with venom. "It'll just get in the way."

I'm keeping it," Tred replied. "What's it to you?" He grabbed the diamond-less fish in in his fist roughly, causing pieces of the sculpture to fall off. He held the fish sculpture like a large child without regard to its well-being.

"Wait a minute. Wait just one minute. I saw this sculpture before, Skid. You remember don't you? We saw this same fish someplace else."

"Hey, you're right," Skid answered. "We saw that fish in that girl's apartment. This must be where she works. Maybe we're getting closer to where we can nab her."

"Do you think she's already left the building?"

"She ain't gone yet, you dummy," he answered. "Her car is still in the parking lot."

Not knowing how dreadfully close they were to finding her, they continued their insidious search, hinting at the cruelly they would enact if they caught her. They were hired to find the diamond, and, so, they continued the hunt as if the rewards would be theirs. They weren't smart enough to realize that when the goods were delivered, their lives would no longer be of any value to the head boss.

Rachel stood in the cabinet frozen in time, shaking uncontrollably and praying that they would not find her. To her utter relief, they began to walk by the cabinet she was hiding in. From the outside, the cabinet appeared too small to house a human body, and so they skipped the cabinet to search from station to station. They threw the lights on, opened doors, and stole items they thought were valuable. Periodically they would menace her, calling out to her as though they were playing a game of hide-n-seek.

"We know you didn't leave, girly. Where are you, girly? Come on out. We're not going to hurt you. But we aren't going to stop hunting until we find you either!"

Rachel remained completely still. If she made any kind of noise, they would find her. Her mind was silently trying to work out an escape plan from the building before they could figure out where she was hiding. She wanted to cry but knew she couldn't. Her sobbing would give away her location. She also knew they would eventually backtrack their steps and likely discover her hiding place upon further inspection. Her hiding time was limited.

She quietly watched them as they left the area to meander through a set of open doors just above the stairway. She could hear sounds of tumult on the floor above her. Things were slammed and dropped to the floor. The noise they were creating gave her a chance to escape, she thought. Slowly she opened the door. Stepping out, she first collected the newly re-fashioned fish that lay hidden in the soft case. She then began walking slowly toward the door that led to the hallway and then out to the guard station.

Rachel could hear the commotion in the room above. The main door was old and it squeaked when it opened and closed. Gently she pushed the door open, hoping that the sound of the old hinges wouldn't betray her. It was no use. She managed to pry the door open and slip through without incident, but as the weight of the door shifted back in the other direction, the hinges let out a silence-ending screech. Rachel was not going to wait to see if the two intruders had heard it. She knew they did because the noise from above the staircase ceased as they strained their ears to identify the noise from the room below.

She bolted for the guard station, hanging tightly onto the bag. She made her way past the other work areas and out through another door, which led to the guard station. Behind her she could hear them running down the staircase and through the door, which again screeched on its hinges. As she approached the guard station, Godfrey was nowhere to be found. Realizing that she could likely not outrun them, she decided to hide behind the guard counter. She was terrified to discover Godfrey lying in a pool of his own blood behind the counter. A knife protruded from his back.

Rachel wanted to cry but her fear drove her on. She could hear them approaching. Beneath the counter was extra storage space concealed by a low sliding door. She thought she could fit, so she slid the doors open and crawled inside, making sure to take the fish sculpture with her. Before sliding the doors closed again, she pulled Godfrey's body close by to help disguise the storage space. She slid the doors shut and held her breath.

The killers ambled down the hallway and walked passed Godfrey, who appeared to be lying as they had left him. They made their way to the office door but the door was locked. Curse words spewed from their mouths at the realization that she might be locked behind the door. They angrily grabbed a nearby chair and smashed the chair through the door window, breaking the glass, which flew in all directions. Skid then reached his long arm through the gaping hole and unlocked the door. The two men then trashed the office in search of Rachel.

Rachel knew she had to move. It was only a matter of time before her assailants made their way back in her direction. She slipped quietly out of her hiding place, avoiding the blood that had collected around Godfrey's body. Once she left the guardroom she made her way to the west side of the building toward the main entrance of the building. She knew that the light switch for the main offices was located nearby. Rachel planned to turn them off so that she could use the dark to camouflage her escape. A great fear was beginning to take hold of her like a giant set of hands tightening around her shoulders. Listening intently, she made her way to the door that led to the main offices. Glass scrunched under her feet, stirring the silence of the guard station to life and making her pause momentarily.

Right on cue, Skid and Tred stopped their commotion. With ears like bats, they smiled at one another as they heard the familiar noise of glass being crushed under feet. They turned and began to walk in Rachel's direction. Their taunts and boisterous laughter preceded them, signaling their approach. Rachel ran quickly down the hallway to the offices, flipping the light switch as she passed. The room went dark, and she ducked behind one of the desks, counting on the total darkness to hide her.

"She's gotta be close," she heard Skid say.

"Hey, girly, where are you?" Tred chimed in.

The darkness slowed them down a bit, but to Rachel's alarm, the storm outside illuminated the room with lightning flashes. Her plan had fallen through, and she would have to run in order to put distance between her and her enemies.

Peter raced to the Glass Design Building as fast as he could travel in a terrible storm. There was no problem parking the car in the almost-empty parking lot. His heart began to panic as he saw Rachel's car still parked where she left it. Not waiting for Tom, he began to walk around the back of the dark building. He didn't even notice that it was raining or that he was getting drenched. Something deep inside started to bother him. Things didn't seem right. He knew Rachel's car was in the lot but he didn't know to whom the other car belonged. Turning the corner, his eyes honed in on a broken window. It couldn't be missed. Stopping momentarily to observe the sharp-edged glass, he bent slightly over and placed one leg in first and then the other. He was thankful that there were no signs of blood. Adjusting to the dark, he slowed his pace being careful not to get caught unaware and to listen for any signs of Rachel. The lightning flashes outside were his only source of light.

He passed by the guard station, noticing Godfrey's dead body lying on the floor. He began to panic, quickening his pace as he approached the old door to the work stations. Carefully, he pushed the door open, causing the hinges to screech—a noise that alerted Rachel's assailants to his presence. The two men immediately turned and, rather loudly, moved toward the door, knocking over several pieces of office equipment in the darkness. The sudden alarm raised between the two men gave Rachel an opportunity to escape. With their backs now turned to her location, she silently began to make her way toward the west wing. But before she took a second step a bolt of lightning lit up the night sky and cast three elongated shadows along the office wall, which Skid noticed. He quickly turned and grabbed hold of her arm just above her elbow.

"Now I've got you!" Skid proclaimed. His foul breath made her nauseous, and his firm grip caused her pain.

Peter heard Rachel scream. He broke out into a run, launching himself from the darkness to deal Skid a solid blow on his chin. The blow knocked Skid unconscious, but before Peter could collect himself, Rachel screamed his name in warning, and Tred smashed an office chair over the back of Peter's head, knocking him unconscious.

Tred then grabbed ahold of Rachel and cruelly pulled her to him. He kicked the unconscious Skid, trying to wake him.

"Get up. Let's get out of here. We've got the girl," he growled.

Slowly Skid got to his feet and rubbed his hurting jaw. As his head cleared, he remembered the blow. He found Peter lying on the ground, and so he drew his foot back and delivered his shoe into Peter's stomach as hard as he could.

Rachel let out another cry as Peter lay motionless on the ground. They dragged her off to the ugly, old, wet vehicle waiting outside. They forced her inside and slid in beside her, watching her every move. With the turn of their key and the shift of a gear, they deviously drove out of the parking lot with a helpless Rachel locked in the back seat.

Tom and Kayleigh drove into the parking lot of the Design Building in the pouring rain. With one glance, Tom instantly recognized Peter's car sitting next to Rachel's. Something didn't seem right, and he became concerned for Kayleigh,

"Kayleigh, you can wait in the car if you like. I'm not sure what I'm going to find in there," he cautioned her.

"Oh, no I won't. I'm going with you," she demanded. "I'd be too afraid to stay out here all alone."

"All right then. Let's go in but let us try to be as quiet as we can", Tom said as he opened the car door and closed it very quietly. He took Kayleigh by the hand as they ran toward the building, trying not to get drenched before they reached the building overhang.

The front doors were locked, and not wanting to give up because of the two cars in the lot, they began to make their way to the other side. It wasn't hard to spot the broken glass in the lightning flashes or see the window was now left wide open. Tom put his finger to his lips so Kayleigh would know not to make any noise. He then stepped inside. Still holding her hand, he helped her step over the open window. Once inside they tried to shake off the raindrops, hoping to stay drier and maybe a little warmer.

It was dark inside but that wouldn't stop Tom from looking. He thought he could find the light switch somewhere by the door as he slid his hand along the wall until he finally located a toggle lever. It was easy to flip the lever upward, allowing a small light on the top of the ceiling to throw dim illumination to this small, abandoned room. The light was exceedingly welcome as they dragged the extremely heavy metal door open and slid a chair between the door and its frame to hold it open, helping the light travel down the hall and faintly into some of the crevasses.

Cautiously, they made their way through another storage room and into the hall that led to the station where the guard desk was located. Kayleigh almost let a scream when she noticed the feet of guard lying there on the floor, but she knew she couldn't because it would warn any intruder of their presence. Tom hurried over to see if the guard was still alive.

Standing upright, he took a step backwards, realizing there was no life left in him. It was at this point that Tom wanted to panic but forced himself to stay in control.

"Come on, Kayleigh. Let's find a phone and call the police. "

Leaving the guard area, they could hear glass popping under their feet as they made their way through the office door. Gradually they walked on as the light seemed to be getting dimmer and dimmer. Tom could barely make out the phone on one of the desks.

"Where's the lightning when you need it?" he mumbled under his breath. He reached for the receiver and shakily began to dial for help.

"Please get me the police. We are in the Glass Design building on 34th Street and someone has been killed. Can you send help right away? We are looking for my sister, who is missing."

It didn't take long for them to stumble upon Peter lying on the floor. They tried to help him as much as they could until the police came. They could hear the sirens in the background getting louder and louder. The police were there in force. Floodlights were all over the place. The police knew where a main switch was and wasted no time in illuminating the entire building. With light, it was easy to see the total path of disarray.

Two officers quickly ran to Tom and Kayleigh and shouted, "You're under arrest!"

And with a swiftness that came before thought arrived, handcuffs were applied to their wrists.

Tom's protests fell on deaf ears. When he realized he was useless to help with the situation, he yelled at the officer to get an ambulance for his friend. Then, he got right in the face of the officer and yelled, "My sister is missing! And what are you going to do about it? We did not do this!"

"That's right," said Kayleigh.

"Fine, replied the officer. " Explain it down at the station."

An ambulance was called for Peter and could be heard in the distance. Tom and Kayleigh stood there helpless. The ambulance arrived shortly after they were called and drove right to the entrance of the building. Making their way into the building, the police officers directed them through the right doors to where Peter lay in serious condition. They checked his vitals, strapped him to the gurney, and then wheeled him to the ambulance. He was in serious condition and, so, was rushed to the hospital to keep him from dying. All the while Tom kept protesting out of concern for Peter and Rachel, but the police officers forced him into the car and took him to the police station where they booked him.

CHAPTER EIGHT

The Searching Continues

Tom was allowed to have one phone so he called his parents, knowing that they were the most able to help them. Once Tom's parents arrived, they applied as much weight as they could on the police department, making it perfectly clear to those in charge that their daughter was missing and that they wanted something done about it. After a good deal of wrangling by his parents, Tom and Kayleigh were finally released from their jail cells and brought in for questioning. The police began to understand the severity of the situation and were now doing everything in their power to help find Rachel. The murder scene was totally roped off. The investigation was now in full tilt. Fingerprints were taken, and the area was a swarm of officers and officials. Godfrey's body was removed and taken to the morgue. His relatives were notified and all the necessary arrangements were being put into place. The presence of the body made everyone fear for Rachel's safety.

Tom was numb inside. The plight of his sister weighed heavily on him. Peter must have the answers, so he left for the hospital as soon as the police finished their questioning. He was pleased that Kayleigh asked to go with him. A group of officers stood outside Peter's room ready to extract answers as soon as he was able to provide them. They were limiting access to Peter and stopped Tom and Kayleigh upon their approach.

"You can't go in there," one of the officers said as he stepped between Tom and the door.

Tom tried to explain to the officer that Peter might be the only person who has answers to his sister's whereabouts, but the officer explained that he would be unable to speak with Peter because he remained unconscious from his injuries.

"If you leave your name at headquarters, we'll notify you as soon as the doctor clears for questioning," added the officer in a conciliatory tone."

Tom thanked the officer and turned to leave, determined to speak with Peter despite the officer's rebuff. He was not going to be denied access to the one person with information regarding his sister's whereabouts. He decided to go directly to the doctor overseeing Peter's care. He found the doctor in the main corridor, reviewing notes with the head nurse in charge of the floor. He greeted the man politely and explained the situation as best he could. He explained that his sister's life may very well be in danger and that Peter may have information that would lead to her rescue.

Sympathetically, the doctor reminded Tom that when last he checked Peter was still unconscious and that an unconscious man can give no answers. Tom's face drained of emotion when he realized that he would have to wait to speak with Peter. Noticing his crestfallen look, the doctor agreed to check on Peter once again and allowed Tom to make the visit with him.

With the doctor at his side, Tom and the doctor walked into Peter's room with Kayleigh just a few steps behind. Several officers joined them. Peter lay there in the hospital bed unmoving. Tom rested his hand on Peter's arm and said his name. The doctor stated that the blow to the head had caused severe swelling in his brain but that he did not think surgery would be needed. Given time, the swelling in his brain should go down and that Peter would likely regain consciousness at that time. He would not be able to answer questions before then. Running through his checklist, the doctor noted that he was resting comfortably and that his vitals looked good. He reminded both Tom and the officers that he would have the nurse call them as soon as he awakened. Until then he was to get his rest.

Tom left his name and number at the nurse's station and reluctantly left the hospital. As they left the hospital, Tom was distant. His eyes were open but they were not seeing. He simply stared into space, failing to even notice Kayleigh's request for his keys. His anxiety was self-evident, and Kayleigh now realized that Tom was in no shape to be alone. She took the keys from Tom's pocket and drove him to his parent's house. They were visibly upset. The FBI was running wiretaps through the phone line, and the main room was overrun by police officers. Tom went right to his mother's side, put his arm around her, and promised they would find Rachel. They both sobbed uncontrollably.

There was such emotion and activity in the house that Kayleigh knew she could leave and would not even be noticed.

Looking around, she noticed a small pad of paper by the telephone and quickly penned a note to Tom. She left her phone number and asked him to call when the time was right. She thanked him again for his help that evening in the rain, and then tore off the page and left it on the table by the phone. Kayleigh walked over to a police officer and asked if he would mind giving her a ride home. He shook his head affirmatively, and they quietly walked out of the house.

Hours passed before Tom realized Kayleigh was not there. His heart sank at the thought of her leaving without him knowing it but he knew she understood. Nevertheless, he panicked at the thought of never seeing her again. He instinctively went to the phone where he found the note she had left. He raced through the words, and sighed with relief when he saw her phone number penned to the paper. He hung onto the note like a treasure. He reached into his back pocket and pulled out his wallet, prying it open. He quickly reread the note again, memorizing her phone number, before gently placed her note inside his wallet. He then picked up the phone and dialed her number. To his surprise, she picked up.

"Kayleigh, I'm sorry," he said apologetically but before he could say more she eased his mind, reaffirming that she understood. "Can you come back?" he asked sheepishly. "It makes me feel better to have you here...as weird as they may sound coming from someone you just met hours ago."

"Of course I'll come," she replied without hesitation.

"I'll pick you up; I'll leave right now," he said. Tom placed the receiver back into its cradle and headed straight to his car.

Meanwhile, Rachel had been taken to a small shack on the far end of the wharf where very few people passed by. Most of the activity was on the other end where the crowds of travelers would gather. Rachel was tied to the chair with a gag in her mouth. She knew she couldn't give them any indication that she would try to get away, so she sat perfectly still. As her captors spoke, she observed and tried to remember every detail that her memory could hold onto. She listened to every word that was said, trying to gain the name of a place or of a person that would be of importance to authorities. Her eyes were scanning the room, hoping to glean some detail that would reveal her location, when they alighted on an object sitting on a dirty little table in the corner of the room.

She couldn't believe her eyes; it was her fish—but which one? Suddenly she couldn't be sure if she had left the fish under the counter at the guard station or if she had taken it with her when she ran. Her mind raced, replaying the whole evening back in her mind like a rewound tape. She wondered if this was the fish with the diamond in its belly. She retraced her steps that evening: She'd had it when she left her station, she'd had it when she went down the hall to the guard station, and she'd had it when she hid under the counter. In her mind's eye she could see the case in which she placed the glass sculpture laying under the counter. She had shoved it into the corner and left it there when she tried to make her escape. If anyone of her fellow workers found it, she hoped that they would recognize the unique fish as hers, and that they would put it in the office until she could claim it. This fish, she remembered, must be the one Tred claimed as his own.

"Okay, my pet, Skid said to her. " Your buddy, Peter, is in the hospital 'cause I put him there with my boot. He's lucky I didn't kill 'em. Now we are going to call his room, and he is going to give us the diamond in exchange for you. Got it?"

The venom in his voice scared her, and she feared that they might harm her regardless of Peter's response. She also knew that Peter didn't know where the fish was. She had taken it to the design factory to repair it. She knew they would hurt her if they did not get what they wanted. Though she was afraid of what they might do to her, she couldn't give up the fish with the diamond so easily. If it came to life and death, she would have to reveal its place but until then she would keep her mouth shut. Maybe time was on her side.

Her abductor tried making the call but was told by the nurse on call that Peter was unable to take the call because he was still unconscious. Angrily, Skid slammed the phone down. A stream of obscenities rushed from his mouth. "The lil' punk is unconscious!"

"How can we get the diamond if he's not awake to bring it here?" Tred queried. "The boss won't like that one bit. He don't like to be made to wait."

Skid didn't bother to reply.

Rachel's heart sank when Skid reported the news from the hospital to his companion but she kept her head together, keeping her head down so as not to draw attention to herself. She tried to remain optimistic, trying to convince herself that Peter would be alright. Instead of worrying, she tried to focus on the immediate danger she was in, listening intently to her captors, and recording whatever information they foolishly disclosed. The mention of "the boss" piqued her interest, but the day's ordeal had exhausted her, and despite her best efforts to stay awake, she drifted off to sleep.

She was awakened by the sound of people talking, which lifted her spirits. Beyond the walls of the enclosure that she was tied up in, she could hear men shouting orders, mothers yelling for their children, and laughter. The commotion made her think that there must be some sort of festival going on outside. There was nothing she could do but sit still and wait. Her restraints were well-fastened, and she had been unable to remove the gag from her mouth. She would have to wait. Perhaps someone would find her. Perhaps Peter would come to her aid.

CHAPTER NINE

The Great Escape

Peter's unconscious state lasted long into the night. Around 3:20 in the morning he was being pulled out of his fatal slumber. He sat up almost instinctively without waiting for his mind to clear. He was confused. Placing his hand on the back of his head, he could feel pain when he touched the spot where he took the blow. He tried to recall the events that brought him to his current state. Rachel suddenly flashed into his mind, and he was overcome with worry. He instantly picked up the phone without a care for the late hour. He called Tom's apartment, but there was no answer.

He slowly raised himself from the bed, which was no easy task. His head was pounding with the rhythm of a beating drum. He applied pressure to his head where it hurt the most and forced himself to stand. He knew he would have a difficult time moving and stood motionless momentarily. He could hear the noise of footsteps drawing closer. It was the sound of a nurse drawing closer. Afraid that she might enter his room, he laid back down on the bed just as the nurse opened the door. She walked in to check his bedside water and to take his pulse. Peter lay there with his eyes closed pretending to sleep. He hoped she would finish what she had to do and then leave, which is exactly what she did. Peter watched with his eyes half closed as she left the room.

Peter's main goal was to sneak out of the hospital without anyone knowing because they would never let him leave. He had regained a little of his strength, finding it a little easier to sit up, but supporting his weight was still difficult. He moved cautiously to the closet door where he grabbed his clothes before returning to the bed. Voices echoed down the hallway. As quickly as he could, he lay back down and pulled the covers up to his neck but he was too late. The doctor and the night nurse noticed that he was awake when they walked in. They greeted him and asked him how he was feeling. He told them his head hurt pretty badly.

"You had quite a blow to your head," the doctor said as he examined Peter's wound. "Quite a few people will be happy you're awake and responding to questions. The police and someone by the name of Tom are very anxious to speak with you."

"It'll have to wait until morning. I'll be able to think a little clearer."

"Alright," replied the doctor as he and the nurse left the room.

As soon as the doctor left the room, Peter slowly got out of bed and moved toward the closet once more. He had left his tie in the closet. He breathed a sigh of relief when he spotted his tie hanging in the closet. His hand instinctively went right to the familiar spot to insure that the diamond was still there. He was relieved to find it still in its hiding spot. He started to put his tie on when he heard another set of footsteps approaching his room. The door was slowly pushed open and a nurse, who was new on the shift, walked in. She reached for a thermometer and put it into Peter's mouth.

"Are you feeling any better?" she asked.

He couldn't answer but nodded his head affirmatively. She took his wrist and felt for his pulse, while looking at her watch. She wrote down the timed results then reached for the thermometer. She recorded the results and left the room as quickly as she had entered. He immediately walked to the door, pushed it open slightly, and peeked out into the hallway. He could see two nurses at their station but could barely hear what they were saying. They talked briefly and then both of them parted in opposite directions. The night nurse that had taken his temperature headed toward his room, and Peter ducked back inside, hoping she did not re-enter. He listened intently for her footsteps as she walked briskly past his room. He then peeked his head back out of the door.

Not seeing anyone at the nurse's station, he stepped out the door and quickly walked across the empty hall. He made his way to the stairway and followed the exit signs out of the hospital. As he stepped out to the curb, he tightened the knot of his tie and hailed a cab. He directed the cabby to take him to the police station.

The sergeant behind the counter asked what he could do to help him. When Peter began explaining the situation, he picked up the phone and called his superior officer. Before Peter knew it there were five officers surrounding him.

"Come into my office," Officer Bailey commanded as two officers snatched Peter under each arm to escort him through the officer's door.

Peter cooperated and answered the questions that were asked of him. He was anxious to find Rachel. No one could comprehend how concerned he was for her. He had to find her, but could not let his mind go there for fear of what it might do to him. The officer offered to drive him back to the hospital. Peter declined but asked for a ride to Tom's house.

Tom was ecstatic to see Peter. The two of them put their heads together to try and figure out a way to find Rachel. Peter asked if the abductors called.

"No," Tom replied. "The police have the phone tapped but no luck. Got any ideas?"

"I have an appointment with Mr. Morgan from the Huntington Museum tomorrow," Peter replied.

"Where are you going to meet him?" Tom asked.

"The Old Tower Café."

"This could be a good opportunity, Peter. Whoever has been ransacking your place and whoever has Rachel has been privy to our whereabouts all along. Perhaps they are aware of your meeting tomorrow and perhaps we can catch them with their guard down. I'll go to the restaurant before you get there and find a seat in the back of the room, so no one will know I'm even there. What do you think?" Tom asked.

Peter smiled.

The next day Tom drove past the Old Clock Café and rounded the corner to park his car in an inconspicuous place. A favored old ball cap covered most of his blond hair. A casual sweatshirt, jeans, and tennis shoes made him look younger and less noticeable. The Old Clock Café at one time housed all the instruments an old clockmaker needed to make timepiece repairs. The big old windows now made the inside look so inviting to any window shopper as they passed by. A huge canopy blocked the sky as it hung over the front area of the building. There was a decorative rod iron fence that circled the entrance area that looked more like artwork then a divider. The beautifully set tables had a single vase flower that sat in the center of each table, which made it look so inviting to any customer.

Walking into the entrance was an adventure to the eye. The inside was adorned with many of the old clocks from an era gone by. Viewing the walls would take your mind back to another period of time where your thoughts would stop for a moment and linger in memory lane. The lovely, thick, artistic woodwork ran along the interior of the room with matching crown moldings raced along the edge of the ceiling. They complemented the handsome old counter that showed its age. Cozy booths with high backs and decorative glass dividers lined the large antiqued room. The tables were remarkably set and just by sight you knew the place was distinctly decorated with impeccably good taste.

Tom had asked for a booth in the back of the room and chose the one that offered a direct view of the whole restaurant. He ordered coffee and sat back to relax, waiting for Peter to enter. He watched the door as it swung open and closed. One person after another entered the café. There was nothing unusual about the first few customers who walked in, but then something about the next customer caught his eye and struck a nerve. He watched the elderly gentleman intently as he entered the café. His eyes were seedy. They scanned the room looking for someone who wasn't there. His face flashed disgust when he realized he'd have to wait. He checked his watch as he rudely demanded a booth by the window, and then ordered a glass of wine.

Peter was the next to enter the café, and the elderly man immediately approached him. Tom thought this odd because Mr. Morgan, if that is who the elderly man was, had not ever met Peter before.

"Are you Peter Armstrong?" the elderly man said, extending his had to Peter.

"I am," replied Peter as he took the gentleman's hand in his.

"I am Mr. Morgan of the Huntington museum," the elderly man said with a smile.

Mr. Morgan gestured to the booth he was sitting at, and the two men sat down to discuss business. Peter scrutinized Mr. Morgan from across the table, trying to assess whether or not Mr. Morgan could be trusted.

"Can you tell me about my grandfather?" Peter asked. Tom sat quietly observing in the distance.

Mr. Morgan described the old house his grandfather loved so much. His description brought to Peter's mind the visit of his youth.

"How did you meet my grandfather?" Peter asked next. Peter turned his head to address the waiter and failed to notice the twitch in Mr. Morgan's right eye that contradicted his otherwise placid face.

"We met years before Nicholas left for Africa and became old friends. Will you be requiring the assistance of the museum to exchange your grandfather's inheritance for monetary funds? Your grandfather explained the entire situation to me at great length before he passed away."

Mr. Morgan's eagerness made Peter suspicious.

"Did Jayba kept in touch with my grandfather?" Peter asked in an attempt to catch Mr. Morgan off guard.

Mr. Morgan was unfazed by the question and recounted the long friendship that Nicholas and Jayba maintained over the years but he quickly asked about the diamonds again. He seemed preoccupied with them, and his eagerness again raised Pater's suspicions.

"My hope is that you've got the diamonds in a safe place," Mr. Morgan asked barely able to contain his curiosity. "Your grandfather said that one of the diamonds alone was worth nearly $1.5 million dollars. The museum is prepared to present you with a check in the amount of $1.25 million dollars—a sum slightly less than market value."

"It is very difficult to keep such an item safe," Peter said as he instinctively reached for his tie. Peter's action did not go unnoticed by Mr. Morgan, who was astutely observing Peter. Mr. Morgan noticed a small lump on his tie that seemed more than a little unusual. He surmised that Peter had at least one of the diamonds stowed away in his tie. Mr. Morgan's satisfaction caused him to drum his fingers on the table, catching Peter's eye.

Mr. Morgan wore a ring on his finger that sparked a memory for Peter. He remembered sitting with his grandfather, and he remembered the physical detail his grandfather had told him about Mr. Morgan.

"Are there many earthquakes where you are from, Mr. Morgan?" Peter asked slyly.

"There are very few," Mr. Morgan responded tersely.

Peter smiled at his response. He knew for certain that he was not sitting across from Mr. Morgan, who had lost part of his finger in an earthquake many years ago. Whoever was sitting in front of him had a complete set of fingers—all of them whole. When Mr. Morgan turned his gaze to his wine, Peter threw a glance toward Tom. Turning his attention back to Peter, Mr. Morgan reached into his vest pocket. Peter winced, imagining that he was pulling out a gun. Instead Mr. Morgan pulled out a checkbook, and Peter let out a sigh of relief.

Mr. Morgan, I won't be selling you the diamond today," Peter interjected quickly. "I would like to meet with you and the board of the museum next week before we make the exchange."

The eyes of the man sitting across the table narrowed. Boiled in anger, but he maintained his composure.

"Very well. I'll notify you of the time of meeting," the imposter said.

They both stood and locked eyes. A tacit understanding passed between them. Both knew the game was up.

"Where's Rachel?" Peter asked abruptly.

"Ah," replied the imposter. "You want the girl. Well I want the diamonds. Looks like we might make a deal today after all."

It was all Peter could do not to attack the man in public, but he knew that if he struck the man, he might not ever see Rachel again. He gave a quick look to Tom, who continued to observe from a distance. But it was too late. Before Peter could get Tom's attention, Mr. Morgan's imposter pulled a small gun on him. Peter glared at the man.

"Where is Rachel, scumbag?"

"Don't you be insulting me or I'll have the diamonds, and you won't have the girl. Now let's take a little ride down to the water's edge. Let's go," the man sneered.

Obediently, Peter turned to leave with the man, but as he did he shot Tom a surreptitious look. Tom was already standing, sensing something was drastically wrong. He nodded to Peter. Peter knew his friend would follow. He didn't want to put him in any danger but had to take the chance because Rachel might be at the end of their ride. Tom trailed them as closely as he could without being detected. He watched as Peter was forced at gunpoint to get into his own car and drive. Tom went to his own vehicle and headed in the same direction, staying inconspicuously behind them.

CHAPTER TEN

The Water's Edge

Kayleigh had spent the day at Tom's parent's house in hopes of lending some help or comfort to his parents. In making conversation she repeated the events of how Tom helped her when the water dammed up on the road and caught them both by surprise. Their concern for Rachel was debilitating. Kayleigh was helping with coffee and food not only for Tom's parents, but also for the detectives who were monitoring the phone taps and securing the family. The hours seemed to go on forever with no word from anyone—when suddenly, the phone rang. Almost in unison all of the heads in the room turned to look at the phone. The detective motioned Tom's father, Ned, to answer the phone and stall the caller as long as he could. Ned had been well-briefed and given specified orders on what should be done in case of a caller. Now was his chance to help find out the answers. All he had to do now was stall.

"Hello, this is Ned Jacobs," he said anxiously and then he went quiet.

"We have the girl," a distant, menacing voiced sounded in response. His words left an uncomfortable feeling in the pit of Ned's stomach.

"We'll offer you all the money we have. Just name your price," Ned replied urgently. Beads of sweat first collected and then ran the length of Ned's forehead.

"That's not what we want," the voice said angrily. "We want the diamond and only the diamond. Have someone deliver it. Get it to us at Wharf 5. Knock four times on door 316 at eight o'clock tonight. Send only one person to deliver it, or you'll never see the girl again. Don't try to fool us; we are watching your every move."

"Wait," Ned begged. "What diamond?"

"That's your problem," the voice asserted. "We get the diamond; you get the girl."

"Please, let me speak to my daughter!" Ned pleaded.

She's all tied up now," the voice said sardonically before breaking off into a chuckle that ended abruptly in a dial tone. All eyes were on Ned as he stared listlessly at the receiver.

Sergeant Crane worked furiously at the phone tap, trying to trace the call.

"Do we have it, Officer Tagan?"

Officer Tagan turned with a puzzled look, "They told Ned 316 on Wharf 5, but they either got it wrong or they lied. My guess is that they lied. It's coming up 318."

"No doubt it's a set up. Wharf 5 is where the cruise boat always docks. There could be hundreds of rooms down there and hundreds of people boarding the ship. We may have a hard time getting through traffic or finding anyone down there."

The decision had to be made regarding who would take the diamond to the wharf. With Tom and Peter already trying to find Rachel, Kayleigh offered to go, knowing Ned was in no shape to make the run. Sergeant Crane asked to speak with her privately.

"You'll be taking a pretty big risk. You'll have to pretend that you have the diamond in your possession. You will be closely guarded and wired. We'll surround the area and overtake them as soon as they open the door. We appreciate this chance you'll be taking. It may lead to the capture of Rachel's kidnappers."

Kayleigh was scared, but eager to help. She was always able to keep fear at a distance and maintain her confidence during the most adverse situations. She also knew not to enter this kind of situation with too much confidence because it might put her in serious danger. She would need to be extremely careful and follow the instructions of the police methodically. But she was inconspicuous looking. She knew that she might be the only one that could get them to lower their guard, which would allow the police to rescue Rachel.

"What do I have to do?" she asked.

The sergeant began to take immediate action. There would be definite protection provided for Kayleigh. Orders were being given to officers—time was of the essence. Backup was called in to cover the delivery, and Kayleigh was given a list of instructions.

She was questioned again and again about the details of her instructors just to make sure that she had memorized them. It was crucially important she got it right the first time for her own safety and for that of Rachel's. She was given orders to go to 316 but not to knock until she turned and saw Sergeant Crane give the signal. When he gave the signal some of the best men in the police force would be ready to act. Hopefully the snipers wouldn't be needed.

Kayleigh drove her car down to docks. The Sergeant and his police staff followed close behind. She had her orders and knew what was expected of her. She was wired with a hidden microphone tucked in her thick, dark hair where it would not be easily found. Kayleigh was very nervous but ready to help out. She squinted her eyes so that she could see through the evening glare. There were people everywhere standing by the dock. The crew of the Capture Cruise Boat was loading luggage while excited travelers scrambled up and down the dock. The air was filled with excitement and the excited chatter of travelers. The noise was deafening. She wondered how this would play out with such a huge crowd gathered at the water.

Kayleigh had a difficult time finding a parking place. Luckily the car she owned was small enough to fit into a spot that a larger vehicle could not squeeze into. Slowly getting out of her car, her eyes searched for anyone who might look familiar. She walked toward 316 confident that the police were there somewhere guarding her. The dock that held the parked cruise ship was old but free of the debris that usually litters a wharf area. An effort had been made by the city to make this a touristy location. New railings and fresh pavement were put in along the dock area. The normally closed little stores that lined the water area were now open with the evening's last minute shoppers.

Kayleigh glanced at the buildings lining the wharf. The structures closest to her were very modern, nice-looking dwellings. As her eye traveled down the row of housing, however, it was clear to see the decline of the once well-kept buildings. Paint that had been applied years ago showed signs of aging. There were patches of raw board where weathering had dealt the buildings a hard blow. As her eye traveled farther along, it was obvious that these buildings were almost totally neglected and in a state of ill repair. She glanced at the numbers and became increasingly uncomfortable. The house numbers on the buildings that she was walking next to read 214 and 216. She was still a distance from her destination, which appeared to be located in a pretty rough part of the wharf. Her stomach tightened. She apprehensively glanced around as she meandered her way to the desolate end of the wharf. She knew she was being guarded and watched and felt safe in their protection but could not identify one of the hiding police officers. Kayleigh thought she would give the system a test, so she whispered, "Are you there?"

"We're right here."

CHAPTER ELEVEN

A Plan Unraveled

There was a small shack just a few buildings down from 318 where Arthur lived. Attached to the small, old shack was a weathered lean-to just big enough to give shelter to Nellybell, Nellybell's pull cart, and maybe some hay. Arthur owned Nellybell—his donkey. But the little donkey was not only Arthur's most loved companion; Nellybell was also his livelihood. Arthur had lived by the docks most of his years. Early in the morning before the warm breeze became hot, Arthur would hook up Nellybell to his four-wheeled cart and they would begin to make the long trek down to the docks as they did every day.

The fishing boats were tied to the big cement posts that lined the dock. Loops of large, thick ropes were pulled snug to keep the small ships from drifting off. The smell of fish lingered in the still air, refusing to leave, searching out the nostrils of any one who happened to be passing by the water's edge. The hard workingmen who pulled the nets were busy categorizing their catch for the day. Most of the fish were sorted and thrown into their proper wire bin where they would wait to be weighed and boxed. The damaged fish were usually thrown on a pile to be

119

discarded but some were left to rot or become food for the birds. Eventually the unwanted fish would wash out with the tide and become food for all sorts of scavenging fish that hungrily waited for their daily, free meal.

Arthur would make his way to that pile and search out the nicest looking fish, wash them off, and lay them on a piece of fresh freezer paper. He would then place his selected wrapped fish on the back of the smoothly worn cart that clearly showed years of continual daily use. When his cart held just the right amount of fish, Arthur and Nellybell would clip-clop their way to the wealthy neighborhoods where Arthur would sell the fish to the rich ladies who spoiled their cats by buying only the freshest fish from him. They wouldn't hesitate to pay the eighty cents for one of his fish. On a good day he was tipped a few nickels. Arthur had a regular route that would lead to the back doors of these houses where he would hand one piece of fish to the hired help in exchange for its worth. At the end of the day, in the baking heat and in the warm evening breeze, he and Nellybell would slowly make their way home. It wasn't much to most people but it was home to Arthur and Nellybell.

On the last day of the week's end they would take a small detour to the shops that lined themselves along the docks. This is where Arthur would buy their food for the following week. The farmers would bring their washed produce to be sold at the little stands that lined the dock near the far end of the street. Arthur would purchase a few fruits and vegetables for himself along with one or two extra carrots for Nellybell. Further along they would stop at another open stand where they sold little bundles of hay, bins of corn, and sacks of oats. Arthur would place one or two clumps of the wrapped hay in the cart, pay the proper amount, and if he had enough money left over from the week, he would purchase a small amount of oats which was always a special treat for Nellybell.

That particular evening Arthur and Nellybell were making their usual trek home. Tired from the long hard day, Arthur allowed Nellybell to mosey along as if they had all the time in the world to traipse through the crowded streets. Arthur may have been up in his years, but this did nothing to hinder his astuteness. Arthur couldn't help but notice the pretty, dark-haired girl walking in his direction. It was very plain to see she walked hesitantly. She kept looking nervously over her shoulder. Arthur scanned the area, looking for whatever it was that troubled the young lady. Concerned, Arthur nudged Nellybell onward past their normal stop.

Peter knew he was in trouble. His abductor had a gun pointed directly at him, so he remained motionless as he drove the car to the docks. Tom, who had followed Peter to the docks, parked his car out of sight before getting out and approaching Peter and the man with the gun.

"Get out of the car," ordered the elderly man with the gun. Peter did as he was told. "Now start walking that way," the elderly man barked as he pointed toward the end of the dock.

Skid stepped outside the door of the shack, holding a loaded gun at his side. He immediately recognized his boss and the gun protruding from his pocket. Skid's mind held only greed and deceit, and he was only ever concerned with his immediate desire. He stood guard at the door ready to take any action necessary to insure his greed was satisfied. If anyone or anything showed signs of intruding upon his business, he was ready to use his gun.

Tom was less cautious. He moved with the agility of a cat stalking its pray. He followed Peter and his captor closely, making sure to remain inconspicuous. Tom watched as Peter and the elderly man approached a large man with a gun, who was standing outside of a shack on the dock. As the three of them spoke, Tom made an effort to duck behind some freight, but he was too late. The man with the gun spotted Tom and followed him with his eyes. Tom knew that he had raised the man's suspicions.

Tom decided it was his time to act. He darted at the three men, hoping to subdue the three of them before they could get a shot off. Just as Tom made the decision to assault the three men, the elderly man struck Peter with the gun, knocking him to the ground and nearly unconscious. At the same time, Skid took aim at Tom.

Arthur saw Skid raise his hand to take careful aim with the gun, and thinking he intended to shoot at Kayleigh, he nudged Nellybell forward into Skid just as the gun went off. Despite Arthur's efforts, the bullet hit Kayleigh in her shoulder. Tom spun around and instinctively ran to her side, ignoring the danger he himself was in.

At the sound of gunfire, the police emerged from their hiding places, and the elderly man yanked the tie off of Peter's neck. He then headed for the shack with the intent of using Rachel as a bargaining chip. Time stopped. Everybody froze as the elderly man entered and then re-emerged from the shack with Rachel in tow and a gun pointed at her head. He had his arm around her neck in a vice-like hold to maneuver her as his shield. He knew by the horrified facial reactions of everyone in view that he was in full control.

The elderly man heard sirens in the distance, setting alarms in his disturbed mind. Calculating the time line he was now on, he knew they were heading right for the docks and then right for him. Fear began to take hold of his very being, pressuring him to move more quickly. He demanded Rachel to walk and to walk fast in the direction of the cruise ship. This was his only means of escape. His immediate plan was to board the cruise ship and blend in with the crowd.

He moved the gun from her head to her side as they walked, forcing it hard into her ribs. He forced her up the ramp and onto the huge ship and out of sight by the excited people hollering goodbyes and yelling off the boat to their relatives and friends standing at the dock. The police officer's eyes intently followed them like eyes in a haunted picture. They watched helplessly as Mr. Morgan cleverly played out his escape plan. They waited in the background, keeping a proper distance, waiting for their chance to pounce. At the moment their main goal was to keep Rachel alive, trapping their prey would come later. Sergeant Crane's well-trained police force was already working on a plan and notified every authority needed to see this through to a successful end.

The elderly man forced Rachel onto the boat amidst the crowds of people, laying low and just waiting for the ship to leave the dock. He nervously checked to see if the tie with its lump still rested in his pocket. Mentally choosing the best place to remain inconspicuous, he rudely nudged her toward two empty seats against the wall and toward the corner. He ordered her to sit down and not to utter one word. "If I go down, so do you," he said menacingly. He threw her an ugly stare. He looked like a caged creature about to attack in defense of itself. His anger made her sink within herself—defeated. After all the anchors were drawn, the ropes lifted and the engine engaged. The big, beautiful ship started to systematically pull away from the dock. No one aboard the ship noticed the tear slowly making its way down Rachel's cheek, nor did anyone on the docks notice the anguish on Peter's face.

In the commotion Skid too had slipped back into the shack. He grabbed the stolen fish that was pilfered from the glass factory and used the distraction that his boss had created to sneak out the back door snake-like. But Sergeant Crane had planned for such contingencies, and Skid found a police unit waiting to arrest him. Each officer had a tight hold under each arm with a pair of handcuffs safely securing his hands, preventing him from escape. Obscenities flowed from his mouth, directed to anyone who happened to look at him. He knew he was done and that he was unlikely to see freedom for a long time.

Kayleigh lay there fighting to remain conscious. The extreme pain caused by her wound kept her from slipping away into darkness. Tom had to keep from crying. His heart was breaking for the girl that had saved his life and put her safety in jeopardy for his friend and sister. An ambulance could be heard approaching in the distance. Tom held Kayleigh's hand, knowing he wouldn't leave her now; he would make this trip to the hospital with her. As he stepped into the ambulance, he remembered his sister, who was still in danger. He was suddenly torn and he moved to step out of the ambulance but Peter caught his gaze and reassured him that he would see to it that Rachel returned home safely. Tom returned to Kayleigh's side as the EMT closed the rear doors of the ambulance.

Peter walked to the shack that had held Rachel captive for the last twenty-four hours. Recognizing her sweater, he walked over to the chair and picked it up. Out of curiosity he exited through the rear of the building where he noticed the glass fish that Skid had stolen from Rachel's work station and who must have dropped it when he was hauled into custody. Peter bent down and grabbed it too, believing it contained the diamond.

CHAPTER TWELVE

Unwanted Cruise

Peter and Sergeant Crane wasted little time as they made their way to the dock station and demanded the cruise ship's security be called. The slow moving clerk nearly had his neck wrung by the two extremely agitated men standing in front of him. Before the Sergeant even had opportunity Peter barked at the clerk to get on the hot foot or there would be consequences he was unprepared to deal with. For his part, the clerk heard the urgency in his voice and hurriedly contacted the captain aboard the cruise ship. The Captain and his crew reacted with professional skill. They held a secret meeting to plan a course of action. He appointed two men to first find, and then keep an eye on, Rachel and her captor. Otherwise, things were to go as normal in hopes of not alarming the gunman and making the situation worse.

Peter and Sergeant Crane questioned the young staff member who was working the ticket counter when the ship departed. Coming short of grabbing him by the collar, they tried to get some kind of an intelligent answer from Roger, the lackadaisical young man, who seemed less than concerned that he was part of a police investigation. Sergeant Crane put his face directly in the front of Roger's face and asked emphatically where the ship would next stop. Unfazed, the boy went to the daily logbook sitting on the counter. Running his finger slowly down the left most column of the schedule, he stopped at row midway down the page before looing up to report his findings.

"Tidal Port," he said flatly. Peter and the Sergeant turned and ran from the station to make preparations.

Rachel and the elderly man sat inconspicuously as dusk faded to twilight. The ocean air chilled her to the bone, making tangible the isolation and fear that gripped her heart. The elder man did not speak. To Rachel he appeared to be an unmoving stone albeit one that threatened to pull her to the bottom of the sea.

Captain Trenten was a sly fellow. The two men he tasked with finding Rachel did and reported her location. Fearing that she may be cold and hungry, Captain Trenten ordered staff to service her and her captor as though she were a normal passenger. He sent his senior most staff member, Della, to execute the plan. Della carried a tray full of assorted little sandwiches and went from passenger to hungry passenger to offer each of them a snack. When she approached Rachel, she maintained her composure aware of the danger that the young woman was in. She politely offered Rachel her choice of sandwich and then did the same for her captor, who looked at her blankly. She then moved on to the next group of people, making mental note of Rachel's disposition.

Captain Trenten kept a continual string of servers working the area of the ship in which Rachel and her captor sat. They were his eyes and ears on the ground and their job was to keep Rachel well-fed and safe. If a staff member noticed anything out of the ordinary or if they thought the elderly man might do her harm, they reported it to the captain directly. Through this routine they were to feed Rachel and get her a blanket to keep her warm.

Rachel thought it strange that the staff was so attentive aboard the cruise ship but took comfort in the libations and the blanket she was able to secure. They sat among families with children playing loudly. In this regard, they were out of place as neither her nor her captor spoke or moved. They simply sat undisturbed until the elderly man poked the gun into her ribs to remind her of the sword that hung over her head.

One little boy was being led along by his mother, who appeared agitated with her young son. One of his hands was clasped firmly by his mother and the other gripped a handful of stones. As he passed her, he accidently knocked his hand against Rachel's leg, knocking a stone out of his hand, which rolled under the chair where she was sitting. Normally she would have said something to make sure the treasured stone wasn't lost to the little boy but in this case she simply remained silent. The stone's sad fate struck her and made her cry. She like the stone had been taken from the hand that cherished her. She and the stone may be lost forever. She did not allow herself to linger on the thought for long. She quickly dried her tears lest her captor have excuse to be rough with her.

She looked over at him, suspecting that he had seen her cry and expecting that she would be reprimanded and threatened, but to her surprise, his chin rested on his chest. He was dozing off. Hope swelled within her. He periodically lifted his head in a start but the interval between his sudden wake up grew longer and longer. Each time he would startle himself awake and look at her before his eyes lids got heavy and his head again slumped down.

Taking a chance, Rachel slowly bent over the arm of the chair. Her hand reached under the seat, searching methodically for the stone that had fallen out of the child's hand. The stone was just out of reach, and she had to stretch painfully over the arm of the chair to reach it. With stone in hand, she slowly sat upright, fearfully glancing at her captor's direction. He hadn't moved. She breathed a sigh of relief but knew the hardest part was yet to do.

Hanging out of her captor's pocket was Peter's tie. Risking life and limb, Rachel slowly pulled on the tie until the knot was free of his pocket. With two fingers she worked the tape that held the tie together until it released the diamond, which fell between her fingers onto the deck of the ship. The sound of it hitting the deck seemed to Rachel louder than thunder. Panic began to penetrate Rachel's soul. She looked fearfully at the elderly man, who continued to snore quietly. Fortune was with her. Her captor was still asleep and the stone had not rolled too far away.

But the job was only half done. Now she had to get the white stone that had fallen from the little boy's hand to fit into the small opening where the diamond had previously been. With the same two fingers she began to work the stone into the opening Peter had cut into the tie. The slit allowed the stone to get through. It was a near-perfect fit. Now she had to pull the tape as tight as she could over the stone, which she did without waking her captor. She then tried to place the tie back into his pocket but the pressure of her hands caused him to stir. She sat back, pretending to sleep.

He looked at her with suspicion but sleep overcame him quickly. She waited for his snoring to take regular pattern before grabbing the diamond from the deck with the toes of her right foot. Curling it in her toe, she slowly pulled her foot back toward her. She dropped the diamond into her shoe, pressing it to the toe and then slipped the shoe back on. Just as she made motion to sit back in her seat, her captor grabbed her arm roughly. He was staring at her with anger in his eyes.

"What are you doing?" he growled.

"Nothing. Just trying to get comfortable," she said, hoping that her voice didn't confess her fear.

"If I find that you've been up to something, they'll be hell to pay," he said as his fingers made their way to the knot of the tie. His fingers paused there momentarily feeling the stone before he sat back in his chair and turned his attention to the night sky. Rachel did the same—her eyes boiled in fear.

Still clutching the fish, Peter followed Sergeant Crane around the dock as he tried to organize his forces and secure transportation to Tidal Port. Time was of the essence; the race had begun. The two of them got in a patrol car and sounded the siren, warning people that they better clear out of the way. As they got onto to the main road, Sergeant Crane dropped the hammer. The police car accelerated faster and faster, throwing Peter back against his seat. Each hill they crested caused the car to catch air. Peter clung to the handle of the door as signs and street markers blurred into a string of light. Slowing down was not an option. They hit the city bridge at top speed. Peter gasped when he realized the bridge was up and anxiously looked at Sergeant Crane, who brazenly yelled, "Hold on!"

Peter felt the car accelerate. He felt his hand tighten around the door grip. He felt his stomach harden. And then he felt the car take flight as the wheels of the car left the pavement of the road. They were airborne for only a few seconds, but it seemed like an eternity before they came down hard on the opposite side. Both driver and passenger lurched violently forward as the front end of the car smacked off of the pavement, causing Sergeant Crane to lose control of the car momentarily. The car careened into the guardrail. Sparks flew, and the sound of metal scarping against metal brought them both back into focus as Sergeant Crane wrestled the car back under his control and again accelerated down the road.

Tom paced an imaginary path outside the emergency room. A secondary worry was now of utmost importance to him. He loved Kayleigh and would not allow anything to prevent him from telling her so. Just then the doctor came through the set of double doors. Tom sent him a look that spoke concern.

"She'll be all right," the Dr. Reynolds said. "We gave her a sedative too help her sleep through the night. You can see her for just a few minutes."

Dr. Reynolds escorted him to room 237 where Kayleigh was resting comfortably. His heart stopped as he stood in the doorway. Taking two steps backwards and out of the sight, he stood there motionless because standing at the side of Kayleigh's bed was a nice-looking man, who held her hand next to his heart. He was slightly bent over her bed and it was obvious that they knew each other very well. Tom couldn't interrupt, so he turned, with his head hanging just a little lower and unhurriedly made his way out of the hospital. He made a quick stop at the police station and then hoped in his car to follow Peter in hot pursuit.

Miles away the police car was showing its better side, working its way down the road at high speeds. However, as they approached a construction zone, they both realized they were travelling too fast. A thin layer of mud had formed on the top of the road. The police car hit the mud with enough gathered momentum to send the car into a skid. Sergeant Crane cranked on the steering wheel, trying to correct the skid but before he could get control of the car, it collided with a concrete pole. The front end of the car collapsed, and the force of the collision sent the car over the shoulder of the road where it came to rest over a fifteen-foot drop. The car groaned as it teetered on the edge. Sargent Crane was stunned by the collision, so Peter moved to the rear of the car to balance the weight in the car. He then opened the rear door by throwing his shoulder with great force into it. Once the door was open, he grabbed Sergeant Crane by the shoulders and eased him into the back seat. He pulled the Sergeant free of the car just as it fell off the edge. To his surprise, Peter still held the fish in his hand.

Sergeant Crane regained control of his faculties and looked at Peter, who was already racing up the hill that the car had careened over to get back to the main road. The Sergeant pulled himself up and joined Peter, who was struggling to get a firm purchase in the mud. With a good deal of effort, they made the hill—soiled and wet and frustrated but alive and ready to continue the race.

With no other recourse, they began walking in the direction of Tidal Port. They hadn't walked far when a car came over the hill, and Sergeant Crane walked to the center of the road wielding his badge in his right hand. Peter and Sergeant Crane ran to the car to commandeer the vehicle. As fortune would have it, the driver was Tom who wryly said, "Been playing in the mud, boys?"

They climbed in the car, and Tom took off toward Tidal Port as quickly as his car would allow.

The new dawn light was beginning to spread its prismatic rays across the sky. Morning was beginning to make its presence known and the bundled up, early risers slowly walked about the ship. The crisp morning air attacked all outsiders. It hunted them down, imparting upon them a bone-penetrating cold and an involuntary shiver. As Rachel sat there in the morning sun, she wrapped herself tightly in the blanket to keep the chill away. She could hardly believe her luck. Scully, the morning waiter, was bringing piping-hot coffee to everybody. You could tell it was hot by the steam that twisted up from the spout of the big, round pot. The aroma of the coffee wafted through the air, inciting every nostril it alighted upon to linger on its fragrance. Rachel was overjoyed when she was handed some of the rich, dark brew. Her hands hugged the cup as she sipped her coffee. She murmured in appreciation.

Next to her sat her captor, who was observing the movement of the luggage. Unbeknown to Rachel and the other passengers, he was deviously planning a way to be rid of her. He knew they were coming to the next stop and that there was a good chance that the police would be there waiting for him. He had one diamond and no longer needed the girl. Now he had to think of a place where he could dispose of her or get her out of his way. His deceitful mind watched the entire procedure of loading and crating the luggage. Suitcases sat stacked at the end of the ship where they waited to be loaded into huge crates. Giant cranes that were secured to the docks then transported the large, fully packed crates to the dock. Member of the crew, who stood patiently waiting for the luggage would then unload the baggage and hand deliver it to passengers, who themselves were waiting patiently though they were eager to get home.

Rachel could see that her elderly captor was irritated. He fidgeted in agitation. Before Rachel could finish her coffee, he threateningly commanded her to stand and slowly walk to the other end of the ship. Rachel involuntarily began to shiver a little but not from the cold. She hung onto one of the blankets as she walked to the other side of the ship, trying not to limp with the pain from the extra baggage she carried in her shoe.

Della noticed they were moving and secretly watched their movement to the luggage area. Alarmed, there was no time to send warning signals to the rest of the crew. Mr. Morgan's imposter held the gun to Rachel's side as he forced her to walk where the luggage was being loaded. He secretly contrived a plan to hide her in a huge crate and then callously leave her there until she was found. He did not care what happened to her in the interim. A crowbar had been tucked into a slot by the crate, so that it could be kept handy for use. He observed its location while studying the activity of the loading crew. His evil eye never left Rachel for a moment as he reached for the heavy tool. She would be the weight that tipped the scale in his favor if the battle ever got foul. Using one hand, he took the crowbar, and pried open a nearby crate. He then reached into the crate, grabbed several bags, and carelessly threw them to one side, making room in the crate for one small person.

Rachel was horror stricken at the thought of what might happen next.

"Get in the box, and if you make so much as a peep, I'll shoot you," he said coldly. "You won't know where I am, but I'll know where you are, so stay put. If you blow this for me, I'll shoot that friend of yours too. Have I made myself clear?"

She felt helpless as she shook her head affirmatively and obediently climbed into the opening. As she was crawling into the huge box, her abductor told her that if everything went as planned, she would probably be taken ashore and that the authorities would likely find her when they opened the luggage crates. He reminded her several times that if she made any noise or drew any attention to herself before she was found, he would shoot the box and anyone else that got in his way. He put the board back and used the end of the crowbar to pound the nails back into place. He snidely turned his head to see if anyone was watching, and when he thought his actions had gone unnoticed, he slid the crowbar into its place and then calmly walked away. Rachel sat there thankful for the blanket and would not say a word until she was off the ship.

The elderly man slyly made his way back to a crowded area, hoping to blend in. Mr. Morgan's imposter didn't have a chance. His every movement was being intently observed. He was totally unaware that he was the main character in this new play. Della and Jill saw Rachel being forced into the crate and thought that she would be protected inside her cage until she was safe on land. They kept a secure distance from Rachel's her captor. Their eyes kept constant surveillance, following his every move.

The imposter reached into his pocket to make sure that the diamond was still there. His fingers searched until they found the hard stone hidden within Peter's tie. He tucked it deeper into his pocket, pushing it further down to secure it in its hiding place for the time being. A greedy smile flashed across his face. He made his way toward one of the ship's restrooms, and on his way, he discreetly bent down to snatch a purse that had been foolishly left behind a deck chair. He searched the purse for mascara and eye liner. Planning to use them for his disguise, he quickly slipped them into his pocket, dropping the purse a short distance from where he found it. Not knowing he was being watched, he made his way to the restroom.

In the restroom he went straight to the mirror, applied the color to his hair. After he darkened his hair with the mascara, he grabbed the eyeliner and darkened his eyebrows. His eyes then zeroed in on a hat that was left hanging on a hat rack by the entrance of the restroom. With the movement of a seasoned thief, he retrieved the forgotten article, placing it on his head. Staring at his new image in the mirror, he bent his neck slightly to adjust the hat rim to cover more of his face. He left the restroom confident that his ruse would work. He glanced nervously about. He could tell the ship was getting ready to dock by the increased activity along the waterfront. He thought it would be easy to just slip off the ship blending in with the crowd and going totally unnoticed. He slowly walked toward the ramp, thinking he had pulled it all off. As he walked, he once again reached in his pocket to look for the familiar stone resting in the tie.

CHAPTER THIRTEEN

The Exchange

Tom easily drove to the dock at Tidal Port. Peter and Sergeant Crane were out of the car before it came to a complete stop. Tom threw the gearshift into park and was right behind them. Sergeant Crane scanned the area and was relieved when he spotted his officers there and ready to act if the situation should turn sour. He pulled Peter aside.

"There is only one way off the ship. The entire force is undercover and hidden from view. They'll be ready to act on any given signal or any sign of Rachel and her captor."

Peter and Sergeant Crane decided to split up so that they could better view the off ramp of the cruise ship. All three of them tried to blend into the huge crowd that was eagerly waiting at the dock for their loved ones to disembark. Sergeant Crane patiently stood behind Tom's car. His keen eyes observed every person that left the ship. Peter stood behind a tree with Tom. They were scanning the crowd, preparing for a confrontation. All three men were at the ready, waiting to act at the first glimpse of Rachel.

As they scanned the crowd, Tom asked Peter why he was carrying the glass fish. Peter explained how he found it when the police arrested Skid, one of Rachel's abductors. He expressed his desire to keep the one remaining diamond he had left close to him—assuming that the sculpture he had in hand had the diamond inside of it. Tom agreed that this was perhaps a good idea. Neither of them recognized the decoy Rachel had crafted. In like fashion, all three men assumed that Rachel remained with her captor and that he would not ditch his hostage, so, they scanned the dense crowd for Rachel and the man Peter and Tom had met at the café. They failed to consider the change of appearance Rachel's abductor had undertaken. Up on the second deck of the cruise ship Della and Jill held the knowledge of who that man was and would have yelled to anybody if they thought there was someone there to hear them.

"How can we let him get away?" Della said to her colleague standing next to her. She nudged Jill and started to wave her hands back-and-forth over her head until Jill did the same. Peter and Tom saw the two women waving their arms and wondered what kind of a signal they were trying to send. First, they searched the area below the women to see if there was someone they were trying to draw attention to. They saw no one but the women continued to wave their arms frantically. Della then began to point in the direction of the ramp. Sergeant Crane was the one that guessed the message they were trying to send. He spotted Rachel's captor preparing to depart the boat. Sergeant Crane stared intently at the ramp. From a distance, Peter noticed direction of Sergeant Crane's gaze and followed his stare to the ramp where recognized the man from the café. Peter launched forward to seize the man but Tom grabbed him.

"We have to be smart about this Peter," Tom said ardently. "We haven't seen Rachel yet. We have to be extremely careful until we locate her."

"I understand. We can't let him get away or we may never find her," Peter acknowledged as he got his emotions under control. His eyes never left the man posing as Mr. Morgan, who was making his way down the ramp.

Rachel strained her eyes to see between the slats of wood. The chains that held the large crate began to tighten as the crane lifted and then transported the crates from the ship to the dock. She could hear the crew fasten the crane hook to her crate. Suddenly, the crate she was in began to creak as the crane hosted it from the deck of the ship. The crane operator had been careless and hasty in an effort to complete his task quickly. As a result, the crate swung back and forth dangerously. Rachel felt her stomach tighten as the crate swung perilously back-and-forth in the air. She was scared, but remembered the warning her captor had given her and stopped herself from crying out.

The crane operator noticed the dangerous movement of the crate and was upset with himself for starting too fast. He stopped the crane boom to stop the motion of the crate, and leaned back in the operator's chair irritated that he would have to wait for the crate to reduce its swing before he could lower it to the dock below. He also hoped his supervisor had not noticed his carelessness. As the operator sulked in the cab of the crane, Rachel grew queasy as the crate swung back and forth like a pendulum.

The temperature in the box was also increasing as a result of the crate sitting in the sun for most of the morning. She grew faint.

"Where is she?" Peter barked. His face showed the stress and strain of the situation.

"I don't know," replied Tom. "Let's hope that she is safe and still on board."

"This waiting is unbearable," Peter said urgently. "Something isn't right. We've got to do something!"

"I agree," said Tom. "Let's go."

Sergeant Crane noticed Peter and Tom's start for the ramp and he signaled for his officers to move in slowly on their location. The man posing as Mr. Morgan didn't realize they were closing in on him until he was face to face with Peter. He immediately reached for his gun, which remained in his pocket. He pointed it directly at Peter, who immediately halted his forward progress. Tom too noticed the bulge pointing in their direction and stopped in his tracks.

"Where is she, scumbag?" Peter said as a single vein in his forehead throbbed angrily. It was clear to everyone in the vicinity that Peter wanted to do bodily harm to the elderly man on the ramp.

"Where's the other diamond?" the elderly man said with venom. His eyes stared coldly back at Peter. The coldness of his gaze made both Tom and Peter worry for Rachel's well-being.

"Where is she?" Peter demanded as he returned the man's cold stare with one equally numb to the consequence of death.

141

Their confrontation on the ramp caused a stir in the crowd. A small circle formed around the three men as the crowd backed away.

"Give me the diamond or you'll never see the girl again."

"How do you know there's another diamond? Who are you?" Peter asked unable to comprehend the man's persistence and the violence he was ready to enact for a stone.

"You don't know me, my boy, but if you must know, I'll tell you. I knew your grandfather. In fact I knew him very well. He was my brother-in-law. I was married to his sister. Ken Johnson at your service, nitwit."

"My grandfather was the most generous man I have ever known!" Peter yelled in indignation.

"He was a troublesome old dotard, but I tolerated him for her sake. But when he discovered those diamonds, he became intolerable."

"But how did you even know he had the diamonds? He kept them hid all of his life."

"He kept them hid from me, fool! I was there that afternoon when the native lady bequeathed to him those two precious diamonds. I was stalking your grandfather with the intent to scare him good for interfering in family business! I saw him take something from the wench and I saw the look of amazement on his face. I knew it was something special, so allowed my curiosity to get the best of me. I followed him back to his house and waited until the old fool fell asleep. Then I rummaged through his pants where I found the diamonds. Before I could take what was rightfully mine, your cursed grandfather woke up and hid what is mine!" His voice grew increasingly agitated.

"They were never yours, Ken. They weren't given to you," Peter said in an attempt to reason with the man.

"They're mine and always have been and now I've got one of them and I'll have the other before we're through. Weigh your choice carefully, my boy."

High above their heads another drama was playing out. The crate in which Rachel had been stowed continued to swing back-and-forth perilously. Unbeknownst to the crew, the chain that held the crate to the crane hook had not been fastened properly, and the weight of the crate swinging back-and-forth was too much for the chain to hold. It came loose momentarily, and the crate began to plummet to the waters below. Rachel felt the crate give way. Her stomach churned, and her body tightened up as she felt herself go weightless. Just as suddenly as it had given way, the chain caught again though the top of crate listed dangerously toward the waters, sending Rachel careening to the bottom corner where she came to rest with a thud. The rattle of metal chain links clanging off of metal chain links and the sight of the crate lurching uncontrollably in the air caused a stir in the crowd, which gasped collectively.

Tom too looked to the crate hanging precariously above the water and then looked back at Ken Johnson, whose face looked confidently self-satisfied.

"You don't have much time, and she has even less," he said coldly. "Where is it?"

It suddenly occurred to Peter what had already occurred to Tom—Rachel was in the crate. His heart broke, and he immediately handed the fish to Mr. Johnson, who looked puzzled at Peter's gift.

"I'm not interested in artwork, Peter."

"The diamond's in the fish."

Just as the fish left his hand, the crate continued its downward fall to the water. The splash was tremendous as the crate hit the surface of the water. It submerged momentarily before popping back up to the surface like a bobber. It sat low and heavy in the water. Peter and Tom looked on in horror as the crate began to fill with water. Peter bolted for the water just as he heard Della scream, "The girl's in the crate!"

He took three giant steps and leapt over the rope railing into the water. He swam directly to the slow sinking crate as it bobbed in the waves. He circled the box, looking for some type of opening. He noticed that plank had a loose nail that had not been hammered in securely. Realizing that this was likely the most vulnerable spot, Peter grabbed the top of the board and applied all of his strength in trying to remove the plank from the crate. He pulled back on the panel, and the slat of wood groaned as its timbers snapped and let loose from the crate. With a crack the plank broke free of the crate, and Peter flung it away from him.

"Give me your hand, Rachel!" he yelled.

She clung desperately to his hand, pulling herself free from the luggage that had fallen upon her and the water that had quickly dowsed her. Peter pulled through the opening in the crate and then wrapped his arm around her. She clung tightly to him as he swam back to the docks. Tom dropped down into the water as they approached to help them out of the water, and the ship's crew threw them a safety line. Sergeant Crane rushed to the water's edge, reached an arm over to pull Rachel from the water, and then helped Peter over the wall. Tom extricated himself from the icy waters. Peter looked at Rachel and asked if she was all right. She replied she was fine, but motioned emphatically for him to help her take off her shoe. She seemed to be wincing in pain.

Are you all right?" Peter asked concerned.

"Yes, but you don't understand."

She reached down and pulled her shoe from her foot. The diamond slid from the toe to the heel, and she winked at Peter, who smiled back at her warmly before signaling for her to leave it where it was hidden. With Rachel safe, Peter turned his attention to Mr. Johnson and the diamond he thought he had given away.

"Which way did he go?" Peter demanded. Tom too demanded answers. Sergeant Crane stopped the both of them short, attempting to sooth their anger.

"You've been through enough. We'll take it from here."

He then motioned for Officer Logan to join them, and then ordered him to drive Peter and Rachel home. Though he wanted his revenge, the feel of Rachel in his arms was overwhelming. He kept his arm around her waist, making sure she wouldn't be taken away again. She put her arm around his neck and smiled at him as she ran her hand down the back of his head. Peter winced momentarily when her hand came to rest on the bump from the blow he had received from Skid's companion. She pulled her hand back quickly and apologized.

"Trust me. I don't mind," he said playfully. "Your hands are always welcome."

Meanwhile, Sergeant Crane, Tom, and Officer Tagan wasted no time in their search for Ken Johnson. They knew that they had little time before he disappeared forever. Sergeant Crane unfolded a map of the area across the hood of his police cruiser and began systematically organizing his forces into search teams.

CHAPTER FOURTEEN

In Too Deep

"I've never been in a police car before," Rachel said as they approached the car.

Sergeant Logan smiled wryly and told the two of them that they would have to sit in the back seat. Peter opened the door for Rachel, and she got it in the car. Peter followed her, and Sergeant Logan asked them where they would like to go.

"To my parent's house?" Rachel asked suggestively.

"I think that would be the best place to go," he replied.

Sergeant Logan started the car and shifted it into gear. He turned the car's heater on so they could all warm themselves on the short drive to the home of Rachel's parents. Peter and Rachel relaxed in the backseat. Both of them hoped that Sergeant Crane had already apprehended Ken Johnson.

Suddenly, a shot rang out, disrupting their tranquility. The back right tire of their car exploded into bits of rubber, causing the car to pivot around in a circle twice like a merry-go-round gone out of control before careening off of the road. Rachel was thrown up against the door of the car, and the door flew open. Rachel and Peter were flung from the vehicle like two rag dolls. They were sent head over heels down an embankment where—as fortune would have it—they came to rest safely on a pile of leaves blown together by the wind. They laid there in shock—stunned at the sudden change in events. Officer Logan was nowhere to be seen. He lay unconscious on the car seat, which was to his advantage because Ken Johnson would have killed him otherwise.

Some distance away Officer Tagan heard the gun shot. "Did you hear that? That was a gunshot," he said urgently to Sergeant Crane, who also had his ear to the wind.

"Get in the car," Sergeant Crane commanded Tom and Officer Tagan wasted no time in getting into the car. Sergeant Crane radioed orders to his men as they raced in the direction of the gunshot.

"Get up and move," Ken Johnson ordered as he loomed over Peter and Rachel. His voice was low, slow, and ugly. Peter and Rachel knew they had better obey or they would have to pay the consequences of their resistance. They slowly got to their feet in disbelief.

Ken Johnson had the look of someone who had gone insane. His face was contorted and ugly and his eyes boiled. He felt he had been double-crossed, and his agitation was evident in his voice.

"Where are they?" he growled. He looked wound tight and jittery like a trapped animal. The sound of police sirens echoed in the distance. He knew that his time was short. "Start walking," he commanded, as he moved and pointed the gun he was carrying at Peter. Terror began to race up and down their spines, numbing their courage, forcing them to stand without uttering a word of objection.

Peter and Rachel walked in silence. They were too afraid to say anything. They knew that Ken Johnson would not hesitate to assassinate one of them. He was no longer a rational man. He seemed distracted and agitated. He roughly handled the two of them, directing them to an old barn that looked black in the distance against the setting sun.

In the past, the farm had been plagued by wild, hungry dogs that fed off of the farmer's chickens. In an effort to outsmart the numerous dogs, the farmer dug deep, wide holes, and then he covered them with branches and leaves. The farmer would then sit back and wait for the wild dogs to entrap themselves. Many unsuspecting wild dogs would find themselves taken out of circulation after falling into one of the deep pits. Ken Johnson had no clue that these traps existed. He waved the gun at Peter and Rachel like it was a long power wand that would magically make them follow his orders.

"Walk faster," he commanded as he poked the gun into Peter's back.

They picked up their pace but struggled to keep their footing on the uneven earth. Their next step was perilous. As Peter put his left foot forward, he fell through weathered branches with a sharp crack. Rachel fell with him, unable to halt her forward progress. Gravity drew them down into the darkness—into a pit that had long ago lost its usefulness. The bottom of the pit was muddy, cushioning their fall. Confused, Peter searched about in the dark for Rachel, who he found stunned but unhurt.

Ken Johnson thought they vanished right before his eyes. It took only a few minutes before he realized they had fallen into a hole. Without a flashlight, he had no way of determining the depth of their earthy tomb. He wanted to shoot idly into the dark pit, but that might kill both of them and he needed at least one to find the diamonds. He held back because the sirens were louder, which meant the police were closer. Knowing there was no way for him to get them out, he did what any snake would do—he just left them there. Before leaving, he snarled a chilling threat, pointed the gun, and delivered one shot into the darkness not caring what target the bullet decided to penetrate.

"Where are they?" he demanded. "I'll not be put off again! Give me the diamonds, or I'll kill you both!"

The penetrating darkness acted as their only shield, and that was only if they didn't move or make a sound. He would have to leave, knowing the police would be closing in soon.

The police car raced down the road at top speed and began to slow only after they caught sight of Officer Logan's car in the middle of the road. By this time Officer Logan was straining to regain consciousness. Officer Tagan ran to his assistance, helping him get into a sitting position.

"I'm okay," Officer Logan replied to Officer Tagan's frantic inquiries.

"Where's Peter and Rachel?" Tom asked as soon as he reached the car.

"Aren't they here?" Officer Logan asked in response.

"No," Tom said impatiently.

"They can't be far, Tom," insisted Sergeant Crane. "We'll search the whole area."

Within minutes there were police officers combing every inch of the area, including nearby buildings. Sergeant Crane searched the area for any sign of Rachel or Peter, but the light was fading and, he could see nothing. There was a terrible uneasiness creeping into the depths of Sergeant Crane's soul. He began to pace in an effort to ease his anxiety.

Not far from where Sergeant Crane was pacing, Tom searched the fallow fields of the farm, fearing that he might find a pair of bodies. Without warning, the ground fell out from beneath his feet, dropping him into darkness. He fell hard but was unscathed. Cursing his ill luck, he began searching in the darkness for a way out of the hole. He feared that if he waited no one would find him. Fortunately, the fading light had prompted him to grab a flashlight out of the back of the police cruiser. He reached into his back pocket and pulled out the small flashlight. He pointed the flashlight straight up to the opening of the hole and began turning the light on and off in hopes of signaling a passerby.

It wasn't long before Sergeant Crane noticed the light. He quickly made his way to the flashing light where he discovered the hole. "Who's down there?" he yelled.

"It's me, Tom. Get me out of here."

"What are you doing down there?" Sergeant Crane asked wryly. "You're supposed to be looking for Peter and Rachel."

"Well, I thought I'd search down here first," Tom said equally playful. "Now can you get me out of here?"

"Hold on," Sergeant Crane assured him. "I'll grab a rope ladder and some flood lights. Chances are there are more of these traps around and I won't have half of my men sitting at the bottom of them. With any luck, Peter and Rachel won't find themselves in similar circumstances. Hopefully they're all right."

It didn't take long to get a rope ladder lowered down to Tom, who shook himself as he emerged unhurt from the pit. Aware of the pits, the officers began carefully searching the fields around the farm. Before long they heard Peter call out for help. Tom and Sergeant Crane were there in an instant to lower a rope ladder down into the darkness and extract them from the pit. When they were safely outside of the pit, Sergeant Crane was eager to discover where Ken Johnson had gone.

"He took off when he heard you guys coming," Peter said. "I'm certain that he thought we would be trapped in the hole and he plans to return as soon as he can. He wants my diamonds."

Tom responded without hesitation, "Let's get you out of here then. We'll be going back to my parent's house. "With Peter and Rachel safe, Tom's thoughts traveled miles away with the speed of an arrow to the hospital room where Kayleigh lay. His heart ached with the thought of another man bending over Kayleigh's hospital bed. Their apparent familiarity upset him. He couldn't shake the thought of another man holding her hand. The brewing storm and the flashes of lightning in the far distance brought him back to reality and the situation at hand.

Meanwhile, police were beginning to swarm at the home of Ned Jacobs. Police were everywhere, phone taps were up and running, and unmarked cars parked around the residence. If Ken Johnson even thought of coming close to their property he would be spotted the instant he came within a half-mile of the house.

Before meeting at Ned's house, the plan was for Peter, Rachel, Tom and Sergeant Crane to stop by each of their residences so they could secure clean clothing. Though Sergeant Crane was uncomfortable with the decision, he allowed it, confident that he could keep the three of them safe. The first stop was Rachel's apartment. As she entered her apartment, her eyes shot to where the fish sculpture normally sat. A look of panic spread across her face, a look that did not go unnoticed by her companions.

"What's the matter, Rachel?" Sergeant Crane asked.

"Nothing," she said as the clouds parted from her memory. Her face relaxed, and she let go of the breath that she had been holding. So much had happened that she had forgotten where she had left the sculpture. She hoped that it was still there, sitting securely at the guard station.

The next stop was Peter's. Once again everyone followed Peter into his rented home. He quickly made his way to his bedroom to find some dry clothes as Tom waited by the front door. Suddenly, a shot rang out from behind them, and a bullet whizzed by Tom's ear, forcing him to duck and the rest of the group to drop to the floor. As he moved to get cover, Sergeant Crane shoved Tom inside and slammed the door behind him. Peter bolted from his room with a look of anguish on his face.

Before they could collect themselves, there was a stream of fire crashed through a window, setting the main room ablaze. Everybody rushed to put the fire out. Peter rushed to the kitchen for water; Tom and Sergeant Crane grabbed blankets to dampen the flames. Rachel too worked to put the fire out, dousing the flames with water from a nearby vase.

During the commotion, Ken Johnson entered the building as silent as a phantom. He stood in the front doorway with a crazed look in his eyes. In his hands he held a flamethrower, which he aimed steadily at the group. He had taken them by surprise, and before they even noticed his presence in the house, he had them at his mercy.

He stood there like a demented animal. Flashes of lightning cast his silhouette across the room and illuminated his wild eyes. The look of hatred on his distorted face sent chills down the spines of everyone in the room. He didn't speak; he glared. They knew they were in trouble. Mr. Johnson slowly turned the gun directly at Peter.

"Where are they?" he growled through clenched teeth. He began to rub the trigger of the flamethrower, which sent a signal to all, that he wanted to waste no time and wouldn't hesitate to set off another fireball—only this time it was aimed at Peter's chest.

"I have what you want!" Rachel yelled, fearing for Peter's life. "I'll get it for you."

She bent over and removed the diamond from her shoe. She then tossed the diamond in his direction. Realizing what she had done, Mr. Johnson turned the flamethrower in Rachel's direction. His face contorted in anger.

"I should have killed you when I had the chance."

Without warning, he pulled the trigger, sending a stream of flame in Rachel's direction. But Peter anticipated just such an action and had already been moving in Rachel's direction when Mr. Johnson pulled the trigger. Peter leaned in and grabbed Rachel's arm, tugging her out of the way. The fire ball spiraled past Rachel's shoulder missing its target and crashing through a window setting a blaze outside.

Mr. Johnson just glared at them unconcerned that he had missed his target. "Where's the other one?" he demanded.

Rachel spoke up before Peter could protest, "I think I know where it is. It's at the glass factory"

"Go to the car," he said coldly.

"If she goes, I go," demanded Peter.

"Get going," he snarled aware that the fire would likely draw the attention of local authorities. He had every intention of shooting Peter when they reached the car. Each step took them closer to the car and Peter's death. Ken Johnson raised his gun and aimed it directly at Peter's back. Peter and Rachel turned in unison when they could go no further and sensed danger from the silence that was creeping in behind them. Rachel screamed when she realized what was going to happen.

Sergeant Crane's faith in his department was not unwarranted. He would have been proud of them if he could have seen an instant replay of their heroic actions. When Sergeant Crane and the others didn't show up at Ned's house, his men sensed something was wrong and went to Peter's house. In response to the fire, his officers surrounded the house. It was imperative they remained quiet and unnoticed. Each officer took their place and steadily watched the scene unfold, waiting for the proper moment to act and making sure they were not too late. Several officers positioned themselves in different locations, hiding behind large rocks or stumps. They aimed their rifles at the entrance of Peter's home, set their scopes, and waited for Ken Johnson to leave the house.

Officer Tagan could see through the window of his police cruiser. He watched as Peter and Rachel were forced toward a vehicle by Mr. Johnson, who was using the barrel of his gun to prod the two of them along. Officer Tagan could see that the fire outside the house was spreading in all directions, lighting up the night sky. The lightning and thunder assisted the police force in their effort to slip into hiding places without being heard.

Rachel screamed when she saw Ken Johnson apply pressure to the trigger of his flamethrower. Her physical response was instinctive. She turned quickly and kicked the barrel of the flamethrower to the side, sending a stream of flame hurling to the ground. The blow knocked the weapon out of Ken Johnson's hands. The fire split the darkness, igniting the grass instantly into a conflagration of heat and light.

Recovering himself, Ken Johnson back handed the side of Rachel's face, a blow that sent her hurling backwards to the ground. Simultaneously, Peter lunged for Mr. Johnson, who sidestepped Peter's attack, striking him hard on the back of the head with his elbow. Peter crumpled to the ground, and as Rachel watched helplessly, Ken Johnson picked up the flamethrower and aimed it at Peter. He knew he no longer needed Peter. Rachel would lead him to the other diamond. But before he could squeeze the trigger and send a whirl of flame to engulf Peter, a shot rang out from the darkness. The bullet buried itself in Mr. Johnson's chest, causing him to drop the flamethrower, clutch his chest, and then fall to the ground never to be feared again. At that moment the skies opened up sending a deluge of rain extinguishing the fire.

Peter picked Rachel up off of the ground and helped her back to the house just as the Fire Department arrived to put out whatever fires the rain had not already stamped out.

"Are you okay?" he asked Rachel.

"I'm fine. Wet but fine," she replied.

I'm afraid to let you go," he said as he looked deep into her eyes. "Every time I let go of you, something awful happens." His face showed genuine concern. He caressed her small hand warmly in his, pulling her closer gently. "Rachel, I've asked you for your hand so many times these last few weeks, only to help you out of trouble, now I want to ask you for your hand again."

Her eyes met his, and her expression softened as the meaning of his words penetrated deep into her soul. She smiled up into his handsome face said in a playful, doubtful tone, "Are you asking me to marry you?"

He drew his face closer to hers, "Yes," he whispered almost inaudibly.

"Well then," she said, "yes!" As she leaned in to gently kiss him.

"What about the diamonds?" she asked.

He looked shamed faced and crestfallen. "You weren't there when I had to relinquish the fish to Ken Johnson."

"Why did you give him one of your most valuable possessions?"

"Well, you are my most valuable possession, and it was an easy trade," he said.

She smiled most tenderly. "Well at least we have one of the diamonds," she said as she walked over to Mr. Johnson's body and removed the diamond she had once carried in her shoe. She then placed the diamond in Peter's hand and teasingly told him not to give it away again.

"I'll try not to," he replied with a wry smirk. "There must be a secret place somewhere in this old house where we could hide a diamond for safekeeping."

"Oh, I love this old house, Peter." Rachel said affectionately. "It's so cozy and warm. I cannot wait to live in this old beautiful house with you. We'll have more than one diamond to hide here though."

"What do you mean? Peter asked puzzled. "I had to give the fish sculpture to Ken Johnson, and who knows where it is now."

"The diamond was not in that fish, Peter," Rachel said with a smile.

Peter continued to look puzzled. His forehead wrinkled quizzically. "If that wasn't the fish that held the diamond in it, then where is the diamond?"

"I made two identical fish statues. Before I was abducted by Johnson's henchmen, I hid under the guard counter. I had to hide right next to Godfrey's body in the storage area under the cabinet. I heard them approaching. They kept threatening me as they walked past, never guessing I was so close. When I thought it was safe to leave my temporary sanctuary, I knew my only chance of escape was to sneak to the other side of the building and make my way to the west door before they detected where I was heading. When I heard nothing from them for a time, I left, pushed the fish to the deepest part of the storage space, and then ran for safety. I didn't make it, obviously, but I bet the fish and the diamond are still there now. The fish you gave Mr. Johnson was a duplicate. Skid's companion took it with him when they threw me in the back of their van. The worst thing that could happen is if the company thought the fish at the guard station was the one I was creating for them to sell at the Design Store."

Peter's face relaxed.

Meanwhile, Tom drove back to his parent's house. The police and detectives were packing up, thanking the Jacobs for their co-operation.

"I think everything will be safe for you now," Sergeant Crane told Mr. and Mrs. Jacobs. Has anyone checked in on Miss Daniels?" he said directing his attention to an officer standing by the door.

Tom's father, Ned, chimed in, "We visited her when she first went to the hospital. She was doing better, regaining her strength."

Tom listened intently to his father's reply—silently hoping that she was well but crestfallen at the thought that her heart might belong to someone else. Ned noticed his son's consternation. As he walked by Tom, he laid his hand on his shoulder and said, "She asked about you and wondered why you hadn't come to visit her."

Tom smiled inwardly. He was happy to hear that she had thought of him. As he stood there pondering his choices, Sergeant Crane approached him to shake his hand and thank him for his help. He noted that he was heading to the hospital to take a report from Kalyleigh, and asked Tom if he wanted to join him. Tom agreed.

Sergeant Crane parked outside of the hospital, and the two of them walked in conversation to Kayleigh's room. The other man that had given Tom such doubt was still there at her bedside. Threatened by the man's presence, Tom entered the room trying to feign indifference. He immediately introduced himself in hopes of appearing important, and confident. Kayleigh noticed his anxiety and smiled.

"Bill, this is Tom—the man who rescued me from the flood waters."

Bill stood from where he was sitting, standing a whole foot taller than Tom. He engulfed Tom's hand in his large mitt and shook it vigorously. Tom shrunk back—his display of confidence undermined. "And Tom," Kayleigh mercifully interjected, "this is Bill—my brother," she said with a smile.

CHAPTER FIFTEEN

The Trade

Peter drove to the Jacob's house the next morning. In his eagerness to see Rachel—his future wife—he nearly ran to the door. No doubt retrieving the other diamond was on his mind as well. He knocked more loudly than he intended. Rachel opened the door, smiled, and asked him to come in and meet her parents. They walked into the living room where her parents were talking to Tom about the events that led to the end of Ken Johnson. Holding his arm, Rachel said, "Mom, Dad, this is Peter."

No one could contain the smiles on their faces. It was clear that the news of their engagement had spread. Tom was the first to say congratulations as he reached to shake his hand.

"So, this is Peter that has caused so much commotion as of late," Ned said with mock indignation. Her father also took Peter's hand and welcomed him to the family. Rachel's mother gave Peter a hug and asked if anyone would like a cup of coffee.

After a short visit, Peter and Rachel wasted no time getting out of there. They drove straight to the glass design center, hoping the retrieval of the fish wouldn't prove to be too difficult. The steps were the easiest obstacles they would encounter that day. They approached the guard station, which was manned by a new employee—likely Godfrey's replacement.

"Hello, Ma'am. What can I do for you?" he asked indifferently

"I left a package behind the counter with Godfrey yesterday, and I hoped to retrieve it."

"Perhaps, you haven't heard, Ma'am, but Godfrey was killed yesterday."

"Yes, I know. I was here when it happened. I was…I am the girl who was abducted."

"Oh, goodness. I see. Well there doesn't appear to be a package here for you," he said politely. In spite of affability, he seemed uncomfortable. It was evident to Peter that he was trying to mask anxiety by appearing authoritative. But he began shifting his weight back-and-forth from one foot to the other, and he averted prolonged eye contact with Rachel.

"Well, it was hidden. Any chance you'd let me take a look behind the counter?"

"Please, take a look. Sorry to hear about your trouble, Ma'am," he said politely as he stepped out of her way.

Rachel walked behind the counter, got down on one knee, and searched out the small hiding place where she had stashed the diamond. There was nothing there. She looked at Peter. The disappointment and worry was evident on her face, and he too grew anxious.

"I'm so sorry, Peter. I left it right here. I don't know where it could have gone. What are we going to do?" She asked Peter

"Something's not right," Peter said. "The guard knows more than he is telling us. Did you notice how uncomfortable he was when you asked about the package?"

"Yeah. I guess so. What do we do?"

"Ask a few more questions," Peter said with a smile. "Excuse me, Sir."

"Yes?" the guard responded. He looked slightly agitated as he looked up from the morning paper.

"Yes. Us again. Sorry," Rachel replied apologetically. "We were just wondering if there was another guard that that had been on duty overnight?"

"No, Ma'am. I'm the only one." His tone was noticeably less agreeable. He lowered his eyes back onto the paper indifferent to her presence.

Rachel could feel the blood rush to her face. Peter too grew angry. They stood there motionless, staring at the guard. The silence grew uncomfortable. "Excuse me," Peter said impatiently.

The guard again looked up at them indignantly. "Yes? How can I help you?"

"Are you sure you haven't seen the package? It is extremely important to me." The agitation in Peter's voice was evident.

The guard grew visibly agitated, and stood up from his seat. He approached Peter, moving his face close to Peter's. "I told you twice now. I haven't seen your package. Now move along before I have to escort the two of you from the building."

Peter and Rachel knew they were suddenly in over their heads and made their way back to the car. As they conferenced in the car, it seemed clear to them that the guard knew more than he was telling; and based on his behavior, they felt he more than likely had possession of the package. They wondered if he knew what he had in his possession. They elected to wait for the guard's shift to end and follow him home.

Later that afternoon the guard left the building and got in a blue pickup truck. They followed behind him closely. They turned when he turned and stopped when he stopped, staying back a short distance so he wouldn't notice he was being observed. He drove up the driveway to a small, gray house. He got out of his car, walked up the few steps, and entered the door and walked inside. They waited until they saw the cleaning lady say goodbye at the door, step out, and close the door behind her. It seemed clear that this was his house.

"I don't want you to get into any more trouble, particularly with someone you work with. It's probably best we let it be," Peter said.

"We cannot just leave the diamond, Peter!" Rachel exclaimed. "If those thugs who took me didn't find the diamond, my guess is that this guy didn't either. He probably just thinks he has a pretty sculpture."

"So what then, Rachel? Should we break into this guy's house? Jail time doesn't do either one of us any good."

"Well, hear me out," Rachel said. "I have an idea. That was his maid, right? What if we returned here tomorrow? I'll simply knock on the door and pretend that I want to sell her cleaning products. Perhaps, I can get a look inside and see if he's got the sculpture." Rachel was adamant; her eyes were wide.

"We've done crazier things lately. Let's give it a go."

The following day they drove back to the guard's house. Rachel was dressed in professional attire, attempting to look like a salesman. Peter thought she looked cute. "I'll be here rooting for you," he said.

Rachel lifted the heavy doorknocker rapped it against the door three times. A cross-looking woman answered the door. Rachel introduced herself as a sales woman and explained that she was going door-to-door in the neighborhood to sell cleaning products. The cleaning lady rebuffed her politely.

"But you'll miss an opportunity to win free samples," Rachel said told her. "I have two free gifts for you today." She reached into her bag and pulled out two cleaning products that she had bought at a store and then removed the labels from. "You won't believe how these two products can make your life easier. Would you like me to show you how well they work? Perhaps a coffee table needs dusting or a kitchen counter needs shining? I'd be happy to show you."

"Free you say?" The cleaning lady took the bait.

"Absolutely free," Rachel said reassuringly.

"Well, my name is Lillian. Please come in but only for a few minutes."

"I won't be more than a minute," replied Rachel. As she stepped into the house, she scanned the room for the fish. Suddenly, there was a large screech from the other room. "What is that awful noise?"

"Oh, it's the owner's pet bird. The darn thing is so loud. I can't wait to get out of here sometimes. Here's the coffee table. Let's see how it works," demanded Lillian.

Rachel cleared the low-sitting coffee table. She took a rag out of her bag and applied the cleaner to the wood. "Now doesn't that look nice?" she asked as she placed the spray can on the table. "Now what about the kitchen counter?" Rachel asked eagerly.

"Hmmm," Lillian intoned. "Follow me."

She walked busily to the kitchen. Rachel lingered momentarily to look for the fish. Looking into the office off the main room, she thought she saw the fish on a bookshelf. The cleaning lady noticed almost immediately that she was not behind her and turned around to glare at Rachel suspiciously. Rachel promptly followed her.

Before she could enter the kitchen, the cleaning lady stopped her. "What are you doing here?" she asked angrily. "Who are you?"

"Pardon me, Lillian. I was distracted by the lovely décor of the living room. Sorry to raise any alarms. I see that you're busy. Here are your samples. Now let me get out of your hair, so that you can go about your business." Rachel spun around and exited the house as quickly as she had entered it.

When she got back to the car, Peter was eager for her report. "He's got it, doesn't he?" he asked.

"Yes. I'm pretty sure I think I saw it sitting on a bookshelf but I am not entirely sure."

"Well there is only one way to find out. We have about ten minutes before the guard gets home. Let's go and do this quickly," he urged.

They exited the car and walked slowly to the side of the house. They peeked through the office window. Rachel poked Peter in the ribs, directing his attention to the bookshelf. Sure enough, the fish was sitting on the shelf behind some books. Suddenly, the next-door neighbor threw open the window and yelled at the two strangers, "What are you doing over there? I'm going to call the police if you two don't get out of here right now!"

Peter and Rachel were taken by surprise. The neighbor's yelling jolted them into action and they quickly made their way back to the car.

"Looks like we need to pay our new friend, the guard, another visit."

The next day, they returned to the security station at Rachel's work. The guard was again on duty. They approached the guard, who was sitting and reading the morning paper. Their body language gave away their agitation and annoyance.

"What is it that I can do for you this morning?" the guard said clearly agitated by their presence.

"You know why we're here," Peter replied.

"Look. You two look like a nice couple, but I told you. I haven't seen your fish. If it's missing, I am happy to help you fill out a report or direct you to Lost and Found. Did you search Lost and Found?"

"I know you have the fish," Rachel replied adamantly.

"Clearly we have some sort of..." the guard started to say but he was interrupted by his intercom. It was Mr. Trundle, calling for security. "You'll have to excuse me," he said with a smug look on his face as he rushed off to tend to Mr. Trundle's request. In his haste he knocked his coat off of the back of the chair, which caused to his nice gold pocket watch to fall to the floor. Peter had an idea.

"Perhaps, we can trade a pocket watch for a fish."

It wasn't long before the guard returned. His irritation at seeing Peter and Rachel at his station was noticeable, and he walked coldly toward them without making eye contact. He noticed his jacket on the floor, picked it up, and then placed it back on the chair. His hand instinctively went for the watch, which he found missing. He searched frantically for the watch, turning every pocket of the jacket inside out. He got down on one knee to search the floor. When he got back to his feet empty-handed, he turned and glared at Peter and Rachel. "Where is it?" he rasped.

"Whatever is it that you're talking about?" Peter replied with a good deal of satisfaction.

"The watch, clown. Where is my watch?" The guard turned red in the face.

"Would you like to trade? A pocket watch for a fish?"

"Thief!" the guard accused loudly.

"Who's the thief, Mr. Dugan.?" Peter said as he pulled at the guard's name tag. "That is your name, right?" Peter asked condescendingly

Officer Dugan stepped closer to Peter. "Be at my house at seven o'clock tonight. We'll make the switch."

"We'll be there," Peter confirmed. His eyes never left Dugan's. Dugan sat back down and turned his attention back to the paper.

As they began their decent of the steps, an approaching gentleman whom Rachel knew well and didn't care much for was beginning the ascent of the same steps. His name was Mr. Phillip Grogan and he was both wealthy and rather fatuous. He made frequent visits to the Glass Design Store and purchased some of the most beautiful pieces. Rachel's problem with him was his smugness and his perpetual desire to brag about his collection. As he was checking his umbrella, he bumped into Peter.

"I'm sorry, my good man," he said affectedly.

Rachel rolled her eyes. She knew what was coming.

"I'll be more careful in the future," he said doffing his hat. "Well I say—if it isn't Rachel, my favorite designer here at the Design Factory."

"Good to see you again, Mr. Grogan. We were just…"

"Hurrying after the passions of youth, no doubt. Well, I won't stand in the way. Have a good day," he said kindly before continuing up the stairs.

As they approached the car, Peter impulsively reached into his pocket to check for the gold watch; it didn't take long for him to realize it wasn't there. "Rachel, it's gone. The watch is gone. I don't have it anymore," Peter said anxiously as he searched his pockets again.

"Everyone at work knows Mr. Grogan was a professional pick pocket and even did time for his crimes. A few items have turned up missing, but we've never been able to catch him in the act. You would have thought he would have learned his lesson by now. I think he has it," Rachel said in disgust.

As they had done with Dugan, they would do with Mr. Grogan. She slowly turned and headed for Grogan's car. Quietly she pulled the handle down, cracked the car door open a few inches, and reached in to free Buddy, Mr. Grogan's dog. The dog was more than happy to be free of the car, and she took him around the corner of the building while Peter waited for Mr. Grogan. Rachel had a good hold on Buddy but when a mouse ran across the sidewalk, Buddy leapt from her arms and darted off around the corner. Rachel's heart started to beat faster; she knew what the consequences of losing Buddy would be. She chased after the dog frantically.

Meanwhile, Peter waited for Mr. Grogan, who soon walked out of the building as smugly as he had entered it. Peter called to him.

"Why yes. You again. What can I do for you, Sir?"

"I think you know what I want. Hand it over," Peter ordered, extending his hand palm upward in front of him.

Mr. Grogan smiled and said, "You can't be sure of anything. You leave me alone, hear me?" He turned and began his walk to his car.

"I'll wait right here in case you would like to talk to me."

Mr. Grogan waved his hand dismissively. Peter watched as Mr. Grogan walked around to the driver's side of his car. Peter watched as he strained his neck and turned his whole body around to get a better view of the backseat. Mr. Grogan's eyes searched every crevasse that was big enough to conceal a small dog. He then re-scanned the entire area in hope of spotting Buddy. He then glared intently at Peter, who pretended to doff his own cap in the distance. A wide grin was on his face.

"Looking for something?" Peter flippantly asked.

"So I am," answered Mr. Grogan.

"Perhaps we could trade a pocket watch for a dog."

Mr. Grogan knew when he was beat, so he reached into his pocket, pulled out the gold pocket watch and said, "Could you be talking about this here watch that I happened to find as I was entering this building?"

"Oh, that's the watch all right," Peter smiled sarcastically. He reached his hand out to collect the timepiece. Mr. Grogan placed the watch and chain into Peter's hand. Peter's hand cupped the treasured item. "Now let me see if I can spot that little brown dog that was here just a minute ago."

"Would you please hurry," demanded Mr. Grogan. Peter whistled, signaling Rachel.

Rachel was frantic; the dog raced in front of her beyond her reach. She thought she might cry in frustration. Buddy chased the mouse into the Design Building in the direction of the guard tower. Rachel followed close behind. Dugan nearly jumped out of his shoes when he saw a dog running toward them. He quickly got out of his chair and made for the dog. As Buddy raced toward him in pursuit of the mouse, Dugan reached for him but Buddy evaded his grasp. Buddy's antics only agitated the guard, who was annoyed by the intrusion. By this time the mouse had disappeared into a crack in the wall, and Buddy stood barking at the opening. This gave Dugan time enough to grab Buddy by the collar and escort him off the property. Rachel then came racing around the corner.

Dugan smirked. "Is this mutt yours?" he asked as he walked angrily to the door.

Peter whistled again but Rachel and Buddy still didn't appear. He was dumbfounded.

"Where's my dog?" Mr. Grogan demanded impatiently.

Suddenly, the door opened, and Dugan tossed Buddy out onto the walk. Rachel followed suit, upset with Dugan for his cruelty. The dog collected itself and then recognized its master. Buddy ran directly to Mr. Grogan, whose face lit up with happiness at the sight of his dog. He then glared at Peter before he walked away indignantly.

That night at seven o'clock Peter parked his car in front of Dugan's house and wished Rachel good luck as he handed the watch to her. She cupped the watch in the palm of her hand, gave it a squeeze, took a deep breath, and left the car.

"I think I'll need it," she replied.

Peter intently watched as she walked toward the front door of the Dugan's house.

Dugan was home and waiting and planning. He wanted his watch back but he really didn't want to give up the fish. He had his hawk out of the cage and waiting to strike.

Before Rachel reached the front door, she heard that same ear-piercing screech she had heard the day before but thought nothing of it. As he opened the door, the hawk swooped down at her head, grazing her cheek with its talons. She screamed as the hawk hovered over her head, pecking at her and squawking wildly. She threw her arms over her head and ducked, but the bird was relentless. Peter saw that Rachel was in trouble from the car and quickly moved to help her.

In her struggle, Rachel dropped the gold watch, which Dugan had hoped would happen. He made a lunge for the watch but Peter made it there first. Dugan was off balance, and Peter gave him a swift kick in the ribs. The blow knocked Dugan to the ground.

"Call off your hawk!" Peter demanded.

Dugan admitted defeat and called off the bird, which landed calmly atop a bookshelf. Rachel dropped to the ground in tears. She had several cuts on her face and hands.

"I'll get the fish," Dugan mumbled.

Dugan indignantly handed Peter the fish; Peter threw the watch at his feet in disgust. Peter then helped Rachel to her feet and led her to the car. Dugan slammed the front door closed behind them. Peter left the fish in Rachel's lap and then returned to Dugan's front door. He knocked on the door, and when Dugan opened it, he belted him square on the jaw. Satisfied that he had addressed Rachel's wrongs, he walked back out to the car and drove home. Dugan sat on the ground teary eyed and nursing his sore jaw.

CHAPTER SIXTEEN

The Worth

The following week Peter received a strange phone call that immediately triggered caution. The gentleman on the other end of the phone claimed to be Mr. Morgan. "Is Peter Armstrong there?"

"Yes," Peter replied tentatively. "This is Peter Armstrong."

"I'm sorry to bother you," Mr. Morgan apologized. "I've come across some unfinished business at my office that has caused me considerable concern. You see, I will be retiring soon, and as I was going through my files, I remembered the letters from your grandfather. He did confide in me about some of his plans for your inheritance. I thought I would have heard from you by now. I have your grandfather's will that needs to be executed. This is a matter of great importance, and I hoped you wouldn't mind that I have taken the liberty to contact you. Would you like to make an appointment to discuss some of the details? Mind you, this is not to pressure you in any way. The decision is entirely up to you. I do have a deed for you from your grandfather and I think it would be best if I put that in your own hands rather than try to send it through the mail."

"How does next Tuesday sound? Let's say around two in the afternoon." Peter was confident that he was speaking to the real Mr. Morgan.

"Yes that will be fine. It will be a pleasure to finally meet you Peter. Are you able to find the museum or do you need directions? "

"I'll have no trouble finding the museum. Thank you," Peter answered. "I also look forward to meeting you."

The following Tuesday, Peter and Rachel took the old, repaired cane with its hidden treasure to the Huntington Museum. The weather was warm and beautiful, which made the decision to take Rachel's car for the drive a must. It was an easy choice to make; her car was a convertible. They drove along the countryside reaching areas that were thickly wooded with miles and miles of forest. The breezy red car looked striking against the dark green forest area. Fear would have disturbed their comfort if the route had not been so well known. The treetops were partly growing over the country road, creating the illusion of early nightfall. This was a drive at its best—tranquil and relaxing. A farmer's clearing was ahead with a flowing stream unhurriedly rolling across the road. It had one of those ancient wooden bridges with the hard oak sides that arched itself over the water. It was a lovely drive until the day took an unexpected twist. They were almost to the museum when the most unforeseen event took place.

Peter stopped the car to wait for a long line of the farmer's geese to cross the road. The car had to come to a complete stop. They got out of the car to stretch their legs. Peter jokingly played with the cane, feigning a limp, a pantomime that made Rachel giggle. Her laughter suddenly stopped when she noticed a large dog stalking them from across the road. It was not quite as big as a St. Bernard, but it looked demented with anger. It was growling at them.

The black, longhaired dog had equally black eyes that had a deadly, unwavering stare. His body remained tense. The hair on the back of his head stood on end. His total concentration was aimed at Peter and Rachel. Rachel thought they were going to die; the dog looked like a small bear. Peter knew any move on their part would provoke an attack. They slowly back stepped to the car but every step they took made the dog growl louder. Peter thought to call the farmer but he was out of earshot. Suddenly, the dog ran at them with its teeth bared. Peter struck the dog with his cane, a blow that sent the dog reeling. Afraid, Rachel jumped back into the car, closing the roof and the windows as she yelled out to Peter to join her.

The dog was not down for long. It immediately launched itself teeth first at Peter, who closed the car door just as the dog's snarling teeth glanced off of the car window. Peter and Rachel breathed a sigh of relief as the dog barked wildly outside the car.

Peter glanced at the cane in his right hand. He held just half a stick. The other half was sitting outside on the side of the road where it had fallen when Peter struck the dog. Peter watched in horror as the dog forgot about the two of them and turned its attention to the cane lying on the ground. The dog picked it up in his mouth and then plopped itself on the ground where he began chewing on the cane.

"Great. What now?" Peter's frustration was evident. Rachel let out a deep sigh.

"It must belong to Ken Johnson," she said flippantly.

The cane seemed to pacify the dog, so Peter slowly opened the driver's side door and stepped out. He thought if he could befriend the dog, he could retrieve the diamond without incident. He was wrong. As soon as his foot hit the ground, the dog swiftly closed the space between them with the intention of biting Peter. Peter hurriedly got back in the car. The dog returned to gnawing the cane.

Peter was quick on his feet. Without hesitation, he turned the car on and drove slowly to where the dog was laying, inching the car as close to the dog as he could. For its own part, the dog simply laid there, indifferent to the car. Peter laid on the horn, provoking the dog to further anger. It stood up quickly and barked madly at Peter and Rachel. Peter inched the car closer, backing the dog away from the diamond. He laid on the horn again, but the dog stood its ground. Peter then inched the car forward slowly so as not to hurt the animal and the dog was forced to take a step back, leaving the cane where he had dropped it. Eventually, Peter was able to crack the car door open slightly and then quickly reach down and grab the cane. He slammed the door quickly just as the dog made a move for his arm. They smiled at each other and then headed down the road.

CHAPTER SEVENTEEN

Delayed Meeting

Peter and Rachel parked in the Museum parking lot, and they walked up the steps to the front entrance, which they discovered to be locked. The farmer's miserable dog had delayed them just long enough to miss their appointment. But before they could curse their ill-fortune, the door swung open. A late visitor was leaving the museum and seemed indifferent to Rachel and Peter's presence. Rachel politely smiled at the gentleman as the two of them caught the front door before it closed and entered the museum. They headed down a hall of offices to their right, hoping to find Mr. Morgan.

Before long they stopped by guard, who intended to throw them out of the building. Rachel smiled broadly, however, and politely explained the situation. The guard directed them to Mr. Morgan's office, which was downstairs. She thanked the gentleman, and they made their way to the lower level.

They walked down the hall searching the names that were posted on each window of every door. They found him hunched over his desk, examining an old letter, stained with years. Mr. Morgan looked up from his desk when they entered the room.

"Peter, I'm so glad you decided to come," Mr. Morgan said politely.

"Is it too late to meet today? We had a bit of an encounter on our way here," Peter said apologetically.

Not for me," replied Mr. Morgan with a huge grin. "Please sit down."

Peter and Rachel sat across from his desk as he pulled out a small pile of papers from an old file cabinet that looked like it had been used for many years. Peter instantly liked this Mr. Morgan, which triggered a memory. He allowed his eyes to wonder to the pile of papers held by Mr. Morgan and then to observe Mr. Morgan's left hand. Peter found what he was looking for. The tip of Mr. Morgan's little finger was missing. Peter's mind warmly traveled back to the years that pleasantly took him back to his grandfather's library where he had learned all of the secrets of his grandfather as a small boy and this last important detail about Mr. Morgan.

"Peter, do you know what you are planning to do with your inheritance?"

Peter explained that he would like to sell the smaller of the diamonds first. He hoped to hold onto the blue diamond for a future day. Mr. Morgan agreed that his was a good plan and he also explained that his grandfather had had the diamonds appraised just before his death. The smaller, clearer of the diamonds was worth a million dollars.

"Did you bring the diamond with you?"

"Yes, I did," Peter replied. He removed the diamond from the cane, and handed it to Mr. Morgan, who asked again if he was sure that he wanted to part with it. Peter said he was though he admitted the last few days had made him more attached to the diamonds than he had been previously. Mr. Morgan looked slightly puzzled.

"Well, good. I'll make the arrangements," Mr. Morgan said. Peter stood to leave. "Oh, please sit for just a minute. There is something else I need to discuss with you."

Peter was puzzled and grew anxious. He looked at Rachel, who was equally concerned. Peter sat back down and watched as Mr. Morgan withdrew a large envelope sitting close to the top of his pile. He handed the letter to Peter.

"What is this?" Peter quizzically asked.

"Read it," Mr. Morgan prompted.

Peter read the letter, which had with it another document. The letter was in his grandfather's handwriting, and it explained how proud Peter's grandfather was of Peter and how much happiness he hoped Peter would have in the time allotted for him. It is also explained the other document, which appeared more legal in nature. It was a deed.

"Your grandfather had me purchase the house you live in from Mrs. Charden," Mr. Morgan said before Peter could finish the letter. "He kept tabs on you, Peter, and he knew how much you liked living in the old house. Well, now it's yours."

Peter sat there starring at the deed, appreciative and sad at the same time. His grandfather had reached from the grave to give Peter another gift. Every gift his grandfather had given had greatly impacted his life and this one was no different. He and Rachel now had a permanent home.

"Your grandfather loved you a great deal, Peter. Here are the new contacts you would have to fill out and sign if ever you decide to sell the other diamond. I will be retiring soon. Your new contact would be my grandson—a transition your grandfather approved of. I will fill him in on a few details before I leave. You would have to have it reappraised but there should be no problem in getting its proper sale amount. Before you leave, I have yet another envelope for you. Read its contents later."

With that, Mr. Morgan bid them well, and they exited the museum. When they got to the car, Peter opened the envelope. It was another letter from his grandfather.

Dearest Peter,

If you are reading this letter, you have already contacted Mr. Morgan and hopefully, the museum has purchased one or both of the diamonds. It gives me great pleasure to know you have a secure future and a wonderful house. Very often I would sit and remember the time we shared, especially when I take my old familiar walks to the places we explored together. Just knowing you for that short amount of time I knew you would be honest and intelligent and that you would learn to live with dignity and character. I knew you would grow into a responsible human being, or I wouldn't have gifted you the diamonds. Because of the great monetary power you now control, you have a great responsibility to do what is always right. So keep God in your heart. Allow him to guide you in all life's decisions. Know that I have always loved you and always be generous.

Until we meet again,

Nicholas Armstrong

CHAPTER EIGHTEEN

Ever After

Rachel and Peter were married. They immediately began settling into that big old house that they both loved so much. Tom and Kayleigh were also engaged and on their way over for dinner. The evening was warm and breezy. Rachel opened the windows to allow the warm breeze to blow through the house. Frogs could be heard croaking, crickets chirping, and if you happened to walk outside, the fireflies could be seen lighting up the night sky.

Peter filled the wine glasses as Rachel served the food. Tom and Kayleigh laughed as Peter told them about the farmer's dog. They toasted the soon-to-be-married couple. Many toasts were made that night to Sergeant Crane, Officer Tagan, Mr. Morgan, and to Mrs. Charden, who had paid for their happiness with her life. Peter would remember her fondly for all of his days.

Dinner conversation quickly turned to vacation plans. Rachel had a gleam in her eye when she asked Tom and Kayleigh if they would like to go on a cruise with her and Peter after they were married. Rachel had a hidden agenda. She wanted to reward the crew of the cruise ship for all of their help, and she wanted Tom and Kaleigh to be there with them.

"Of course we would love to go," Tom piped in after seeing the excited look of approval on Kayleigh's face. Peter smiled at the light heartedness of the evening. Now it was his turn to throw a surprise out there and not even Rachel knew what it was.

"I have an errand to run tomorrow. Would anyone care to join me? " he asked with a big grin running from ear-to-ear.

"Where are you going?" Rachel asked inquisitively.

"Are we invited?" Tom asked equally suspicious of Peter's intentions.

"You're all invited," Peter said happily. "But let me tell you where we are going before you agree." His grin got wider. "Last week I had a wonderful idea as I was passing the local real estate office. I went in looking for a small farm with a nice little house and a small barn close by. "

"But we love this place, Peter," Rachel said confused.

"It's not for us, dear. It's for Arthur and Nellybell. If not for those two, we might not be laughing together tonight."

Kayleigh became very serious and was deeply moved by the wonderful gesture. "Yes," she said, "I would love to come along and meet Arthur and his wonderful little donkey. As I understand it, I owe them my life."

"I'm the most thankful," Tom said as he leaned in and kissed Kayleigh on the cheek.

They toasted Arthur and Nellybell. The anticipation for tomorrow brought them great joy that night, and they conversed late into the night. After cleaning up the dishes, Tom and Kayleigh left for home. Peter and Rachel sat side-by-side on the couch in front of the slow-burning fireplace. The flames filtered an orange, warm glow throughout the room that chased away the darkness. Peter sat with his arm around Rachel. The glass fish sat on a bookshelf next to the fire. It would be safe there until it would be needed.

Peter had a hard time falling asleep that night and he sat in front of the fire for a long time, thinking about his life, his grandfather, Rachel, and the family he hoped to raise with her. Before long he grabbed his grandfather's letter and read it again, as he often did in these moments. He pulled his chair closer to the fire so he could more easily read its contents. He eyes alighted on a phrase that had become etched in his heart. "Always be generous," he read aloud, and then he laid the letter down on the chair and went to bed to snuggle close to Rachel.

The End

ABOUT CHERIE RASHEL

Wisconsin has always been home to Cherie Rashel, with beautiful Lake Michigan as a part of the stunning scenery she enjoys daily. She's always delighted in gardening, and has a small lemon and grapefruit tree in her kitchen full of delicious, edible fruit.

Cherie writes with a large audience in mind, and hopes that her work appeals to a wide variety of readers. Her ultimate goal is to present an enjoyable experience to all who read her work.

She married her college sweetheart before she began a career in education, and they have two sons who are active in their family business.

CPSIA information can be obtained at www.ICGtesting.com
Printed in the USA
LVOW04s2234081214

417901LV00021B/324/P